D0046877

Terrible Typhoid Mary

Terrible Typhoid Mary

A True Story of the Deadliest Cook in America

Susan Campbell Bartoletti

Houghton Mifflin Harcourt
Boston New York

www.hmhco.com

The text of this book is set in Bembo.

Library of Congress Cataloging-in-Publication Data
Bartoletti, Susan Campbell.
Terrible Typhoid Mary: a true story of the deadliest cook in America / by Susan Campbell Bartoletti.
p. cm.
Includes bibliographical references.
ISBN 978-0-544-31367-5
1. Typhoid Mary—1938—Juvenile literature. 2. Typhoid fever—New York (State)—New York—History—Juvenile literature. 3. Quarantine—New York (State)—New York—History—Juvenile literature. 4. Cooks—New York (State)—New York—Biography—Juvenile literature. I. Title.
RA644.T8B37 2015
614.5'112092—dc23
[B]
2014023057

Manufactured in the United States of America
DOC 10 9 8 7 6 5 4 3 2 1
4500537401

For Bambi —S.C.B.

CONTENTS

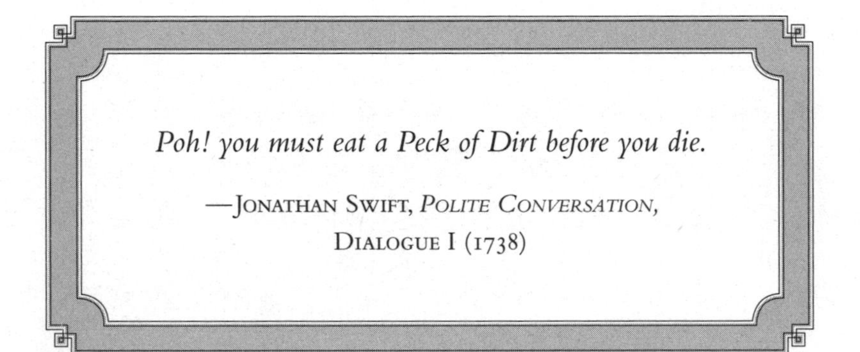
Poh! you must eat a Peck of Dirt before you die.

—Jonathan Swift, *Polite Conversation*,
Dialogue I (1738)

Dear Reader,

If you're squeamish and don't like to read about germs, then you should stop now and find some other book to read.

If you don't scrub your hands with soap and hot water for at least thirty seconds after using the toilet and before eating, if you don't clean underneath your fingernails, if you don't sneeze or cough into a tissue or your elbow or your shoulder in order not to spray germs, if you touch doorknobs or share eating utensils or set your sandwich down on the cafeteria table, if you practice the five-second rule, if you don't change or launder your bath towel at least twice a week, if you don't wipe your cell phone and keyboard with a disinfectant once a day, if you don't clean out your backpack or your purse every day, then read on.

Sincerely,

the author

Mr. and Mrs. Charles E. Warren, their four children, and five servants lived in this graceful-looking Oyster Bay house during the summer of 1906. *Courtesy Oyster Bay Historical Society.*

Mrs. Warren hired Mary Mallon as her cook. The servant's agency said Mary had impeccable references. New York American, *June 30, 1909. Courtesy New York Public Library.*

Chapter One

IN WHICH MRS. WARREN HAS A SERVANT PROBLEM

In Oyster Bay, Long Island, Mrs. Charles Elliot Warren had fired her cook. It was August 1906, and with several weeks left in the summer, she needed a cook. She could not manage without one. Not with a household of four children and five servants to feed. Not with a social calendar filled to the brim with dinner parties and Sunday teas.

For a wealthy woman such as Mrs. Warren, it was a terrible fix. There were plenty of servants in America —roughly 2.3 million—but for women like her, a *good* servant was hard to find.

Mrs. Warren needed a cook who wouldn't mind the lack of freedom and the fourteen-hour days. She needed someone available morning, noon, and night. Someone who wore a white servant's cap and apron, a plain dress, and thick-soled shoes. Someone who never left the house without permission. Some cooks shared rooms with other servants. Others made themselves comfortable sleeping in the attic or the cellar.

A good servant wasn't uppity. She knew her place. If a servant was smarter than her employer, she never showed it. She was humble. She ate in the kitchen, using the plain crockery and ironware, not the good family china and silver. Even though her employer called her by her given name—Bridget or Sally or Peggy or Maggie—she said "Mister" and "Sir" and "Miss" or "Mrs." and "Ma'am." No matter her age, she was always a girl and never a lady.

A servant never used the front entrance of the house. She entered and left through the service entrance at the rear of the property or under the front stoop. If she happened to spy her employer outside the home, she averted her eyes and never acknowledged her.

Good servants understood that all Americans were equal, regardless of class. But they also understood that employers were more equal than servants. A good servant didn't complain. She didn't demand a labor contract with clearly defined hours, duties, and wages.

For many employers, a good servant meant a specific race, nationality, and religion. Some employers hired white help only. Some preferred black help only. Some hired Protestants only. Some hired Catholics. Some hired immigrants. Some would not.

The duty of hiring servants fell to the "lady" of the house, and so Mrs. Warren did what most other New York City ladies did. She telephoned Mrs. Stricker's Servants' Agency on Twenty-eighth Street in Manhattan and said, "Send me a cook."

The agency director gave Mrs. Warren the name of a good, plain cook named Mary Mallon and praised her references, character, and abilities in the kitchen.

No doubt Mrs. Warren was impressed. Mary had worked for some of the most prominent and socially elite families in New York City—families whose names appeared alongside the Warrens' in *Who's Who* and in the society pages of the *New York Times*—and for this she was well paid.

As a cook, Mary earned forty-five dollars a month (roughly $1,180 today). This was much more than Mary would have earned cooking for a middle-class family. This wasn't unusual. The wealthier a family, the more they paid—as much as double the salary for the same worker in a middle-class home. It was a simple fact of life.

Was Mary a perfect servant? No servant ever was.

If she were, she would have been bolted firmly to someone else's kitchen floor long before she had a chance to cook for the Warrens.

There is no record of the interview between Mrs. Warren and Mary Mallon. There likely was no interview. If Mrs. Warren didn't like a cook, she'd simply send her back.

When the agency sent Mary Mallon, she was thirty-seven years old, unmarried, with no family or children, and in good health, never sick a day. She had good references that praised her. Sure, Mary never stayed longer than a year or two at one house, but this wasn't unusual for a servant. Sure, there were gaps in Mary's employment history, but this, too, wasn't unusual for domestic workers.

Mary was Irish and Roman Catholic. Although some employers were prejudiced against Irish Catholics, by 1906 this attitude was changing, especially regarding Irishwomen. More than 80 percent of Irish-born women working in America toiled as domestic servants. Employment agencies touted them as excellent workers.

Many employers agreed. They praised their Irish servants for "quick wit" and "strong arm and voluble tongue." They called their servants "industrious," "pious," and "chaste." They noted that Irish servants had "sterling integrity" and were rarely in trouble with the law. One employer put it simply: "The Irish are, as a rule, honest."

Did Mrs. Warren hold these stereotypical views? We don't know. But we do know she hired Mary on the spot.

Mary's life was about to change forever.

Chapter Two

IN WHICH THE WARRENS GET MORE THAN THEIR JUST "DESSERTS"

Mary Mallon packed her belongings and traveled by train to Oyster Bay, a popular vacation town on Long Island. She found her way to a large yellow house with tall windows and graceful arches and a wraparound porch at the corner of East Main Street and McCouns Lane.

The house sat on ample, well-manicured grounds that sloped down to the bay. It stood at the edge of town, just before East Main Street curved into the woods, hugging the shoreline as it passed other mansions. Mr. Charles Elliot Warren had rented the house for the summer.

A cook's life wasn't easy. But here, there was no dingy flat on the Lower East Side, where immigrants like Mary lived. There was no sweltering city heat and crowded streets and noise and squalor.

In Oyster Bay the smell of ocean was so strong you could taste it in the air. On sunny days, sailboats bloomed in the harbor. Fishermen pulled soft clams from their sandy beds. Seagulls wheeled overhead and complained and then rose up and wheeled and complained some more.

As Mary settled into her new job, no one cared that she kept to herself and spoke little, for she kept her hands and fingers busy in the kitchen, showing off her culinary skills. Hand-cranked rotary beaters and peelers made some tasks easier, but she did most of the work by hand—the mixing, the rolling, the kneading, the beating, the paring of vegetables, the slicing of apples and peaches. Cooks like Mary also washed dishes, swept and scrubbed the kitchen and storeroom, and cleaned and polished the stove.

If Mary knew why Mrs. Warren fired the previous cook, she never said, and probably never asked. Some who knew Mary called her "intelligent" but "non-communicative." They also said she had a "violent temper" and could silence a person "with a glare."

Mary never talked much, and never, ever talked about herself or her past. She kept to herself, minded her own business, and tended to the matters of the kitchen. These were the traits of a good servant. A good servant didn't wag her tongue about her employers. What happened in the house stayed in the house. It was better that way.

✠

Each morning, Mary rose early, never later than six a.m. She emptied her chamber pot into the servants' outdoor privy and washed her hands at the cold-water tap in the kitchen. With no hot-water faucet, she kept water heated on the stove. She used an all-purpose store-bought bar soap that she also scraped into the wash water for dishes. The harsh soap turned hands red and raw.

Once the stove was lit and the dirtiest work done, Mary changed into a clean cotton dress, pinned her hair into a tight knot, and donned a clean white cap. She looped her white cook's apron around her neck and tied it around her waist. She lined up her bowls and spoons and knives and other cooking utensils on the wooden worktable. She had eleven mouths to feed, including the Warren family and their five household servants. An early start to the day was the only way to get the job done.

It was hard work to prepare all those meals, morning, noon, and night, and even harder when the Warrens entertained guests and threw lavish dinner parties. Before breakfast, a cook was also expected to clean the hall, the entrance, and the dining room.

Even though the house was large, the kitchen was probably small. A well-appointed kitchen of the time had a gas stove—by 1906, one-third of all homes had replaced their coal and wood stoves with gas. It had a sink with a counter or drain board, a wooden worktable, and an easy-to-scrub linoleum floor.

Some kitchens had cupboards, but most had open shelves and a large piece of furniture called a "kitchen piano." This was a tall wooden hutch with a wooden work surface and drawers and cupboards for holding sugar, flour, salt, spices, milk, eggs, and molasses. Extra provisions were stored in the kitchen pantry.

There were no refrigerators or freezers. A porcelain enamel-lined icebox usually stood on the back porch. Here, the milkman could easily deposit the milk and the iceman could leave a block of ice. The ice cost about five cents (as much as $1.43 today) for fifteen pounds. The ice lasted up to several days, depending upon its weight, the outdoor temperature, and how often the icebox was opened.

The cook ruled the kitchen. Mary ordered the food—and made sure nothing was wasted. She used the freshest ingredients. Meat from the local butcher. Bread from the local bakery. Fruit from nearby orchards. Vegetables from town gardens. Milk and eggs and butter from a nearby dairy. With these items, Mary made delicious roasts, moist cakes, smooth puddings, and her specialty—homemade ice cream.

Thrift was an art. Though the Warrens didn't worry about money—Mr. Warren was vice president of the Lincoln National Bank in Manhattan and a banker to the Vanderbilts, one of the wealthiest American families—a good cook found a use for every leftover, every crumb.

Bread was dried and grated into bread crumbs for puddings and stuffing and to thicken meat gravies. Toast was transformed into griddlecakes and bread pudding. Meat bones flavored bean soup. Leftover vegetables were added to the soup pot. Fish and potatoes were fried in steak drippings. Sour milk was curdled into cottage cheese. Leftover potatoes reappeared as potato cakes. Not even eggshells were discarded: they were used to clarify, or remove the sediment from, broth, jellies, and coffee.

✠

One Sunday, about three weeks after Mary's arrival, she poured fresh cream and milk and sugar into the inner metal chamber of an ice cream maker. She packed the barrel with ice and salt and cranked the handle. After several minutes the cream mixture churned into smooth, creamy ice cream.

She cut up fresh peaches and folded them in, too. That summer, the peaches were especially sweet and succulent. "The largest and finest peaches that have been shown in town this season," boasted a local orchardist in the *Long-Islander* newspaper.

Mary scooped the ice cream into dishes and set the dishes on a serving tray. A maid served the dessert to the Warren family. That night, there was enough for everyone, the family and the servants. Even the gardener would get dessert. Ice cream was the perfect end to a summertime meal, as it required no cooking. And no matter how much you've eaten, there's always room for ice cream.

The Warrens and the servants may have oohed and aahed about the dessert, something Mary served in nearly every household where she worked. They may have also gossiped about the orchardist. So proud of his peaches, he had presented a basket of them to President Theodore Roosevelt, who was summering a few miles away at Sagamore Hill.

After the dinner party Mary prepared her work for the next day. She washed up the plates and dishes, scrubbed the pots and pans, hung up the jugs, cleaned the stove, and put everything in its place.

Perhaps, before retiring to bed, Mary stole a moment to stand on the huge wraparound porch. Perhaps she breathed in the briny scent of the bay that stretched all the way from Long Island Sound to the Atlantic Ocean. Perhaps in that moment she allowed her mind to travel back to Ireland, from where she had emigrated alone as a young teenager.

To her employers and fellow workers, Mary never spoke of her growing-up years. Most of what we know about her comes from a few documents, from what others say about her, and a six-page letter written in her own hand.

From Mary's death certificate we know that she was born on September 23, 1869, in Ireland. Her parents were John Mallon and Catherine Igo.

From other records we're told that she was born in Cookstown, County Tyrone. In 1883, sometime before or after her fifteenth birthday, she boarded a steamship and sailed to America. She lived in New York City with her aunt and uncle. They died not long after her arrival, leaving her alone in a new country as a teenager.

We don't know why Mary left Ireland, or whom she left behind. We know that her parents survived the Great Famine of 1845 to 1850, a time when the potato crops failed and one million poor people died from starvation or starvation-related diseases. In Northern Ireland, County Tyrone lost at least 10 percent of its population. Most counties lost much more. Perhaps Mary hoped for a better life in America.

We know that Mary could read and write and do sums, as could 73 percent of her peers in Ireland, where the literacy rate was 10 percent below that in the United States. We know she could sew and crochet. She did all of these things well.

We don't know how Mary learned to cook. In New York City, she probably started out in smaller homes, first washing clothes, then ironing and cleaning. We know she was extremely proud of her work. Her employers called her a hard worker and often took her on vacation with them so that she could cook for them.

From later accounts, when Mary worked in a hospital children's ward, we know that she liked children and they liked her. "Often the children will have no one else take care of them when they are very sick," Mary told a *New York World* reporter.

We don't know why Mary distanced herself from

her Irish past. Was she escaping painful memories? Was she escaping shameful memories? Whatever her reasons, perhaps distance helped her cope, manage, and survive.

We know that Mary never lost her lilting Irish brogue, though it softened over the years. It was a part of Ireland she carried with her always, the only part of her past she revealed to others.

✠

In Oyster Bay, Mary settled into a daily routine, preparing elaborate meals for the Warren family and less elaborate and less expensive meals for the servants.

One day toward the end of August, nine-year-old Margaret Warren felt too tired and listless to run and play with her sister and brothers. She complained of a headache. Her mother touched her cheek and noticed that Margaret felt warm. She was running a fever and suffering from diarrhea.

More than likely, Mrs. Warren didn't worry at first. Summer diarrhea in children was a common problem, according to a popular advertisement. "All that is necessary is a few doses of Chamberlain's Colic, Cholera, and Diarrhea Remedy, followed by a dose of Castor oil to cleanse the system" promised an advertisement in the town newspaper. The remedy was available for just twenty-five cents from a local pharmacy.

Over the coming days, as Mary stirred the soup and peeled carrots and potatoes, as she mixed puddings and cakes, as she sliced peaches and early apples, Margaret grew worse.

Her fever persisted, spiking as high as 105 degrees and causing delirium. The maids pressed cool cloths to the little girl's forehead. They may have plunged her into a cold bath to bring down the fever. But Margaret's lingering cough grew deeper, and a headache pounded her skull like a hammer.

The little girl's diarrhea grew bloody and foul. With each bout, the maids stripped the beds and hustled the soiled sheets downstairs to be laundered. Mary kept pots of water boiling on the stove. Someone—the maids or a laundress—scrubbed the sheets and hung them to dry. The maids ran upstairs with fresh sheets.

And then news of the telltale skin rash flashed through the house. Right away, Mrs. Warren sent for the doctor.

The doctor confirmed the diagnosis. Margaret was stricken with typhoid fever—a highly contagious, deadly intestinal disease that killed one out of five victims.

In 1906 there was no immunization to protect people from this disease—a vaccine would not be discovered until 1911. There was no cure. Antibiotics wouldn't be discovered until 1942, and an antibiotic specifically for typhoid fever—chloromycetin—wouldn't be developed until 1949.

All the Warrens could do was treat the symptoms and wait and hope and pray. If Margaret survived, she would have natural immunity to the disease.

Within the week, five more people fell ill: Mrs. Warren, Margaret's older sister, two maids, and the gardener. Two were sent to the local hospital. Local doctors treated the others.

Convinced that the drinking water was contaminated—the most common cause of the disease—the Warrens packed up and hurried back to the safety of their townhouse on the Upper East Side in New York City. Margaret's two brothers were sent to stay with relatives in New Jersey until the danger passed.

Mary Mallon didn't follow the Warrens to their brownstone home. Perhaps her services as a cook were no longer needed. Perhaps she found a better offer. Perhaps she feared that she would catch the terrible disease herself. Perhaps she considered it terribly bad luck that typhoid fever broke out in so many households in which she worked.

What Mary's reasons were, we don't know. We won't ever know. She never said. Mary was private and minded her own business.

She expected others to do the same.

Chapter Three

IN WHICH THE USUAL SUSPECTS ARE QUESTIONED

For the rest of September, the elegant Oyster Bay house stood empty, its curtains drawn, its doors locked. With the gardener sick, the grass grew high. The hedges went untrimmed, the flower gardens untended.

At the end of the month, the house owners, Mr. and Mrs. George Thompson, returned to Oyster Bay. The house was one of three properties they owned. They often rented it out for the summer months while they vacationed at their cottage in the Catskill Mountains.

It was clear that the Thompsons had missed the article in the *New York Times,* for the news about the Warren family had made the front page on September 11, 1906. "Five Ill in One Household," said the *Times.*

So when summer ended, the Thompsons had expected to find the Warrens gone. They didn't expect to find their house the center of a typhoid fever epidemic and their trusted gardener stricken with the disease. Thank goodness, the gardener was pulling through and expected to make a full recovery.

The Thompsons were shocked. Typhoid was not a common disease in wealthy Oyster Bay. It was associated with filth and with people who had careless toilet and hygiene habits. These things didn't describe the Warrens, who surely had clean habits.

But the *New York Times* article didn't blame the Warrens or their servants. The article blamed the house, saying, "It is supposed the water supply was bad." That alarmed the Thompsons.

As landlords, the Thompsons knew that the stigma of typhoid fever would make it difficult—if not impossible—to rent the house again. Worse yet, if the house was sick, if it had an underlying problem that couldn't be resolved, it might be condemned or even burned down. It was a rare and drastic measure, but sometimes deemed necessary in order to remedy the problem and protect the public's health.

Right away, Mr. Thompson contacted the local health department, whose officials were just as concerned.

✣

By 1900, scientists, medical doctors, and health officials had accepted the germ theory of disease. This theory proved that microscopic organisms invisible to the naked eye—germs—caused diseases.

The most common cause of typhoid was water contaminated with the deadly *Salmonelli typhi*. These bacteria could live for weeks in water or dried sewage. When a typhoid victim used the toilet, the infected urine and stool were passed into outdoor privies or flushed into a cesspool. If precautions weren't taken—if a privy wasn't cleaned out, if the cesspool wasn't draining properly, if human waste wasn't disposed of properly—the bacteria could leak into the water supply.

From there, a bacterium could easily make its way into a human body. Just one sip of tainted water or one bite of a tainted fruit or vegetable was all it took for the bacterium to find its way into the intestines and make someone sick.

Knowing this, the health department officials got busy trying to determine how the *Salmonelli typhi* had infiltrated the Warren household. Was it possible that sewage from the stable or cesspools or outdoor privy had leaked into the well, contaminating the water supply?

They poured fluorescein into the second-floor toilet that the Warren family used, and then they turned on the water faucets in the bathroom and in the kitchen below. If water from the faucets turned orange-red, they would know that the toilet plumbing leaked, contaminating the rest of the water in the house.

The water ran clear.

The inspectors pulled on tall rubber boots and gloves. They slopped around both cesspools and the stable, collecting samples. They lowered an instrument into the outdoor privy used by the servants and collected a sample there. They collected more samples from the well, the water storage tanks in the attic of the house, and the kitchen and bathroom faucets. They sent the samples to a laboratory.

As the health department awaited the laboratory results, the inspectors continued their investigation. Was it possible that a deliveryman carried the bacterium on his boots? Had milk come from a contaminated dairy farm? Had the family eaten tainted fruit or vegetables? These were also likely suspects because contaminated water might have been used to irrigate or wash the fruit and vegetables.

But the inspectors ruled out these possibilities. Nearly every family in Oyster Bay purchased their milk and cream from the same dairies, and no other family was struck. The inspectors ruled out raw fruit and vegetables, too. No one had eaten these things at the time of the outbreak.

Again, no other Oyster Bay family had fallen ill. If milk, fruit, or vegetables had caused the outbreak, the epidemic would have been much greater.

The laboratory results came back. Nothing. No harmful bacteria were found in the water, the privy, or the cesspool.

Meanwhile, the *New York Times* reported that Mrs. Warren was better and that "Miss Margaret Warren was getting on as well as could be expected." This must have been a relief for the Thompsons and the health department officials.

The investigation had been thorough. Since no other outbreaks had occurred at the time, and no other outbreaks followed, health department officials determined that the outbreak was a mystery—and it would remain a mystery. The danger had passed. Case closed.

Except it wasn't.

Not for Mrs. Thompson. The Oyster Bay house had been a wedding present. She wanted the problem solved.

Chapter Four

IN WHICH AN EPIDEMIC FIGHTER HUNTS FOR A CLUE

As the days passed, Mrs. Thompson fretted. The local people were gossiping about her house. Even though health inspectors had examined every nook and cranny, even though every test had been performed, even though every test result had come back negative, even though the health inspectors had closed the case, the townspeople continued to speculate that the water was bad.

Fall turned to winter, and Mrs. Thompson worried about the next summer, wondering if she'd be able to rent the Oyster Bay house. Who would risk renting a property where six people could have died from typhoid fever? She had to clear up the mystery, once and for all.

Then came a lucky break. Through friends, the

Thompsons were introduced to Dr. George A. Soper, a sanitary engineer who was considered an expert epidemiologist. He called himself "an epidemic fighter."

Soper was known for his expert study of typhoid epidemics. He had investigated typhoid outbreaks in Boston; Ithaca, New York; and several other cities, with much success. During one investigation Soper evicted two typhoid patients and their families from their home and ordered the house burned down.

Mrs. Thompson must have felt a glimmer of hope, for she hired Soper. Perhaps this man could solve the mystery—without burning down her house.

✢

The Thompsons' new acquaintance wasn't a medical doctor. He wasn't a health professional. He wasn't even a scientist.

George Albert Soper was a thirty-six-year-old sanitary engineer who worked for the United States Army Sanitary Corps. He had graduated with a doctoral degree—a Ph.D.—from Columbia University's School of Mines. He liked to read medical articles and books and was especially interested in epidemiology, a science that studies the patterns, causes, and effects of disease.

Throughout the United States, city governments were hiring sanitary engineers like George Soper in order to improve living conditions and public health and to try to prevent epidemics.

Cities needed help. In 1900, for example, experts estimated that the average New Yorker threw away at least 160 pounds of food each year; 1,200 pounds of ashes from stoves and furnaces; and 100 pounds of miscellaneous items such as shoes, furniture, and other junk. And that wasn't all. New York City had more than 100,000 horses. Each horse dropped an average of twenty to thirty pounds of manure and as much as four gallons of urine each day. Without street cleaning, sewers, and regular garbage removal, this garbage, rubbish, and filth was left in the streets to rot. It eventually wended its way into the drinking water, contaminating it and spreading disease.

Something had to be done. Working with city governments and city health departments, sanitary engineers designed apartment houses with better ventilation and flush toilets. They designed massive sewer systems to dispose of human waste. They planned public waterworks to supply safe, clean drinking water. These improvements helped reduce the incidence of typhoid disease by sixty-seven percent.

But for an ambitious epidemic fighter like George

Soper, 67 percent wasn't good enough. It meant that the danger of an epidemic still existed. And he had the numbers to prove it. In 1906, the same year as the Warrens' outbreak, New York City counted 3,467 cases of typhoid fever. That year, 639 people died. And so when Mrs. Thompson explained her dilemma and asked for help, Soper listened.

The sanitary engineer had many reasons to decline. It would be a difficult investigation. Weeks had passed since the outbreak. The Oyster Bay house was vacant and the victims long gone.

It was a small case, too, for a man with Soper's experience and reputation. But he had a curious mind, and the case intrigued him, so he agreed to investigate.

✠

Right away, Soper headed for Oyster Bay. He arrived at the Thompson house and rolled up his sleeves and got to work.

An epidemiologist works like a detective, gathering information from all types of sources to determine how disease spreads and how it can be controlled and eradicated. Soper retraced the steps of the earlier investigators, hoping to find a clue they overlooked. He tried to create a logical reconstruction of how the outbreak had occurred.

Soper began with the possibility of contaminants that might have been brought into the house from an outside source. Just as the earlier investigators had, he ruled out the possibility of contaminated milk, fruit, and vegetables.

He collected samples from the faucets, the well, the water storage tanks, the cesspool, and the privy. He sent the samples to the laboratory for testing. The test results were all negative.

"I was disappointed," said Soper later about these results. "They [the investigators] had done their work thoroughly. Try as I could, I could not find anything wrong."

Perhaps the house itself was sick. Looking into the house's history, Soper learned that one case of typhoid had occurred there five years earlier. But since then the house had been rented out continually. No further outbreaks had occurred, except for the people in the Warren household.

That ruled out the house. He turned his attention to the Warrens and their habits. Even though he had ruled out contaminated milk, fruits, and vegetables, he felt certain that the infectious material must have been brought into the house, carried by a person or a piece of food.

Might some clue have been overlooked?

He reviewed the facts and found a clue. The Warrens were extremely fond of soft clams. They often bought clams from an old woman who lived in a tent on the beach not far from the Thompson house.

Soper searched for her but was unable to find the woman. With the advent of winter, she had rolled up her tent and left. He inspected the beds where the clams were harvested, and he made an important discovery. "They were sometimes taken from places where they were polluted with sewage," he noted.

If the water was polluted, the clams were also polluted.

But it still didn't make sense. If clams were responsible for the typhoid outbreak, Soper asked himself, why was the disease confined to one house? Most townspeople, it seemed, were fond of soft clams bought from the same woman or harvested from the same bay.

Soper pressed further and found that the Warrens hadn't eaten clams after July 15. Margaret Warren didn't fall sick until August 27, forty-three days later.

Because typhoid fever has an incubation period of ten to fourteen days, clams could not be the culprit.

It was frustrating, but Soper remained convinced that the disease had been carried into the house. But how? And by whom? If it wasn't the water or the milk or fruit or vegetables or clams, if it wasn't the privy or cesspools, who or what was it?

Soper turned over the facts again, focusing on the month of August. He considered the order in which the disease struck: first nine-year-old Margaret fell sick, then the two maids who attended her, then her mother, then her sister, and finally the gardener, who had worked at the house for several years. It wasn't simply the Warrens *or* the servants, noted Soper. It was the Warrens *and* the servants.

This was significant. Because of the progression of the disease, Soper felt certain that no one caught typhoid fever from Margaret. Each case, his instincts told him, was unique and caused by whomever or whatever had infected Margaret.

George Soper traveled to the Warrens' home on New York's Upper East Side and interviewed them. He asked if anyone had left Oyster Bay for any reason. If so, he reasoned, that person may have become infected somewhere else and brought the disease home.

But no, the Warrens told him. Not one family member had gone away. Not one servant. Not for a visit, a picnic, or any other reason.

Except.

The cook who had been fired. She had left Oyster Bay the first week in August and never returned. In her place, the Warrens had hired a new cook. This cook came with good recommendations. She had worked for some of the finest families. She began work on August 4. Her name was Mary Mallon.

Soper counted back the days in his head. Mary Mallon had begun cooking just three weeks before the typhoid epidemic broke out. "Here was by all means the most important possibility in the way of a clue," Soper later wrote in medical journals.

It was a clue because the new cook was the only factor that had changed in the Warren household. Soper pressed further. What sort of meals had the new cook made?

At last he learned that the Warrens had eaten raw fruit after all. The new cook had made a special dessert—homemade ice cream with fresh cut-up peaches. It was delicious. She served it on Sunday, August 20, just sixteen days after she arrived.

As a sanitary engineer, Soper knew that freezing

didn't kill bacteria. All freezing did was make germs cold.

He also knew that the intestinal tract—a coiled, sausage-like tube that measures five feet long in an adult—is an ideal place for germs to grow. Once the bacteria-laden ice cream slides down your throat and moves from your stomach into your 98.6-degree intestines—a temperature at which bacteria thrive—the typhoid germs have found a warm, dark moist environment in which they thrive and multiply. That growth happens quickly and profusely: one single bacterium cell can grow to eight million cells in less than twenty-four hours.

"I suppose no better way could be found for a cook to cleanse her hands of microbes and infect a family," Soper later wrote.

Soper put the facts together this way: the seemingly healthy Mary Mallon had a gallbladder and intestines teeming with typhoid bacteria. "No doubt her hands played a part in it," he wrote. "They became soiled when she visited the toilet, but whether from her urine or feces I had no way of knowing."

After using the toilet, Mary had failed to wash her hands carefully before handling food, Soper conjectured. The bacteria from her urine or fecal matter were still on her hands or under her fingernails. In the act of peeling the peaches and cutting them up and churning the ice cream, she transferred the bacteria to the dessert—and then served it.

This reasoning led Soper to believe that the cook was to blame for the typhoid outbreak in the Warren household.

In his articles, Soper depicts Mary as a cook who had unclean habits. What Soper doesn't say is this: If Mary was infected with typhoid germs, it was nearly impossible for her to wash her hands well enough to eliminate the germs. She would have needed to scrub her hands—front and back, between her fingers, and under her fingernails—with soap and 140-degree water for a minimum of thirty seconds. Water that hot can cause a third-degree burn in just five seconds.

"If this woman could be found and questioned," said Soper, "it seemed likely that she could give facts from which the cause of the epidemic could be ascertained."

It wouldn't be easy to locate the missing cook. Weeks had passed since Mary Mallon quit the Warren household. Her present whereabouts were unknown. Soper had no address. He had no telephone number.

But Soper had her name and description: Mary Mallon, a tall Irishwoman, now thirty-eight years old, with clear blue eyes, a determined mouth, and a firm chin, who appeared to be in perfect health. And he knew the Manhattan agency from which she had been hired.

He intended to find the cook, even if it meant wearing out his shoes.

Chapter Five

IN WHICH THE COOK RULES THE KITCHEN

George Soper's hunt for the missing cook began. His first stop was Mrs. Stricker's Servants' Agency, where Mrs. Warren had hired Mary Mallon.

The agency, it turned out, was owned by a man, not a woman as its name suggested. The director didn't know where Mary was, but he gave Soper a list of seven families for whom Mary had worked. It wasn't a complete list, for Mary had used several different agencies over the years. Sometimes she didn't use any agency, but found work through advertisements.

The list was a start. Like a detective trying to solve a mystery, list in hand, Soper pounded the city streets, knocking on the door of one former employer after another.

To an epidemic fighter such as George Soper, the mystery wasn't whodunit. The mystery wasn't Mary's whereabouts, although that was important too. The mystery was where Mary Mallon had worked as a cook and if anything unusual had happened in the home while she was employed.

Soper was building a case against Mary Mallon.

✣

George Soper had a theory. As a sanitary engineer with an interest in disease prevention, he knew the work of Dr. Robert Koch, a famous German bacteriologist who had proved that specific germs caused specific diseases. Koch had also proved that germs were contagious. His laboratory methods, known as Koch's postulates, are still used today.

By 1900 scientists had found that a small percentage of people who had recovered from infectious diseases such as diphtheria, cholera, and typhoid—and otherwise seemed perfectly healthy—could still transmit the disease. These people were known as "healthy carriers." They had no idea that they were spreading germs.

In 1902 Koch published a paper on the subject of healthy typhoid carriers in Europe. Three years later he won the Nobel Prize in Physiology or Medicine. But the concept of healthy carriers was still unproven in the United States—until now.

George Soper was certain that he was hot on the trail of a healthy carrier, the first to be discovered in America.

If he was right, this discovery would make his career. He would become famous in medical and scientific circles. He would be invited to speak about his discovery at conferences. He would write articles. His name would go down in medical history alongside the names of famous scientists such as Robert Koch.

But first he had to collect the evidence to support his theory. He began with locating the families on his list: Mary Mallon had worked in Mamaroneck, New York; New York City; Dark Harbor, Maine; Sands Point, New York; Oyster Bay, New York; and Tuxedo Park, New York.

Soper interviewed each employer, the family members, and the servants. With dismay, he realized that most employers didn't know much about their servants' backgrounds.

"Few housekeepers seem to know anything about their cooks," Soper later explained to readers of the

Military Surgeon, "much less recall thc food which they have eaten weeks and months ago."

The false clues and the faulty memories felt like a conspiracy to Soper. "Sometimes it appear[ed] that persons were deliberately refusing to tell what they knew," he wrote. "Servants who had been associated with her never gave any help."

No one, it seemed, was inclined to help the sanitary engineer, especially not servants who had worked with Mary. They had closed ranks around her. Why were they protecting her? Was it because they liked her? Was it a sense of loyalty toward another servant? Was it because they feared her? Or because they had taken an immediate dislike to this snooping man?

At last Soper's interviews were completed. As he studied his notes, he made a thrilling discovery. In nearly every household on his list, there had been an outbreak of typhoid fever. There was only one exception, Soper later explained to a group of medical doctors, "a family that consisted of two people of advanced age and one old servant."

Otherwise, Soper noted, the disease did not discriminate between classes. It affected employers and their families and their servants. "In every instance the families have been of ample means and accustomed to living well," said Soper. "In each household, there have been four or five in the family and from five to seven servants. Four of the persons attacked have been laundresses. Two have been gardeners, permanently attached to the country places where the typhoid has broken out."

Each time, the source of the typhoid fever had been blamed on some other cause. A visitor. A new laundress. A footman. Bad water. Bad milk.

In all, Soper tallied twenty-two victims, including the Warren family. In one instance, when nine members of a household were stricken and no one was left to care for the sick, Mary had pitched right in, working side by side with her employer, the wealthy Manhattan attorney J. Coleman Drayton.

"Mr. Drayton told me that when it was over he had been so grateful to Mary for all the help she had given him that he rewarded her with fifty dollars in addition to her full wages," wrote Soper later in the *Bulletin of the New York Academy of Medicine.*

Why didn't Mr. Drayton fall ill? According to Soper, Drayton was naturally immune because he had had typhoid earlier in his life. The same was likely true of the elderly couple and their servant.

Mysteriously, Mary escaped illness in every case

and always left soon after the outbreak. "She had never been suspected," said Soper.

Until that moment.

Soper tracked Mary to an old-fashioned, high-stooped house at 688 Park Avenue. There she cooked for Mr. Walter Bowne and his family. She had begun to work for the Bownes several weeks after leaving Oyster Bay.

But the discovery of Mary's whereabouts came too late. Typhoid had already struck Effie, the Bownes' twenty-five-year-old daughter and one of the family servants, a laundress. "The only child of the family, a lovely daughter, was dying of it," said Soper.

The total number of victims now stood at twenty-four, including the Bowne daughter, who would become the first fatality. "I felt a good deal of responsibility about the case," explained Soper later. "Under suitable conditions Mary might precipitate a great epidemic."

Determined to confront the cook, George Soper paid Mary a surprise visit in the kitchen of the Bownes' Park Avenue townhouse. He felt confident that once she understood that she was infected with typhoid germs, she would want medical help.

"I was as diplomatic as possible," wrote Soper later.

"But I had to say I suspected her of making people sick."

We don't know the exact words that Soper used. He may have been too blunt, for later he admitted to readers of the *Bulletin of the New York Academy of Medicine* that he had bungled the interview. He had made Mary defensive and indignant. "I had made a bad start," he wrote.

We don't know if Mary knew the term "germ theory" or if she'd ever heard of Koch's postulates and the notion of a "healthy carrier." We don't know if she understood that microbes invisible to the naked eye cause disease.

Soper's words may have sounded preposterous to her. How could a healthy person make someone sick? Soper's accusation must have struck at the very core of her sense of self-worth. Mary took great pride in her work. She kept a clean kitchen. She herself was clean.

Mary's reaction surprised Soper. Instead of sharing his concern, she grew angry. She told him that she had never had typhoid. She had never been sick, but had nursed those around her who were sick, helping them through the terrible disease.

George Soper pressed on. "I told her if she would answer my questions and give me the specimens, I would see that she got good medical attention, in case that was called for, and without any cost to her."

Specimens, Mary must have asked. What sort of specimens?

And then Soper told her that he wanted specimens of her urine, feces, and blood. No doubt this felt like a highly unusual, very personal, very humiliating request.

Soper forgot the old adage that cooks rule the kitchen. He didn't notice the anger that flashed across Mary's face. He certainly didn't notice the carving fork lying on the table.

But Mary did. She swore at Soper, grabbed the carving fork, and lunged.

"Apparently, Mary did not understand that I wanted to help her," said Soper.

And he ran.

Chapter Six

IN WHICH MARY WALKS MORE LIKE A MAN THAN A WOMAN

George Soper fled. He raced outside through the basement door, ran through the tall iron gate at the front of the property, and didn't stop until he hit Park Avenue. When he recounted the incident, Soper didn't say whether Mary chased him with the carving fork—and if she did, how far he ran—but he did say, "I felt rather lucky to escape."

Soper was not a large man. One year younger than Mary, he was of average height and had a slender build. Bitterly, he explained that Mary was a large and very strong woman. "She was five feet six inches tall," he said. "Mary had a good figure and might have been called athletic had she not been a little too heavy. She prided herself on her strength and endurance."

He went on to say that Mary was "at the height of her physical and mental faculties" and that she had used rough language.

Her behavior shocked Soper. It also hardened his attitude toward her. In his worldview, no true or proper woman would act the way she did.

Many people from the middle and upper classes would have agreed with him. The dominant social view at this time held that a proper woman should be "pious, pure, domestic, and submissive."

Mary did not fit this ideal. She was strong and tough. She had a temper. She swore. She threatened him.

Soper concluded that Mary Mallon was more like a man than a woman. "Nothing was so distinctive about Mary as her walk, unless it was her mind," he said. "The two, her walk and mind, shared a peculiar communion. Those who knew her best said Mary not only walked more like a man than a woman, but also that her mind had a distinctly masculine character."

It's true that Mary was a strong woman. She wasn't submissive. She was stalwart and brave and not afraid to stand up for herself, even if it meant a fight. She had crossed the Atlantic Ocean alone as a young teenager. When her aunt and uncle died, she fended for herself in a large, foreign city. She had probably done lots of hard domestic jobs as she worked her way up to the station of cook.

In 1907 society had strict ideas about womanhood and marriage, too, based on something called "the middle-class ideal." This ideal said that a proper woman should be married and have children. That she should be a good mother and the foundation of the home. That she should not work outside the home. That she should tend to the needs of her husband and children. That the welfare of society—and even the fate of a nation—depended on her.

A woman like Mary didn't fit this ideal. Like most Irish immigrant women living in New York City at the time, she wasn't married. Neither were more than 50 percent of women her age who were living in Ireland. Young girls and unmarried women were encouraged to emigrate. As a cook, Mary earned more than other domestics, but she would never earn enough to become a middle-class woman.

Mary needed her job. She needed her wages. She wasn't going to let George Soper harass her at her place of work or interfere with her livelihood.

✠

George Soper didn't consider these things, or if he did, he dismissed them. To him, Mary was unreasonable.

As an engineer, he liked to solve problems. Once he presented the facts of the case, he expected Mary to understand the problem and to agree with him. "I expected to find a person who would be as desirous as I was for an answer," he wrote later.

Mary's reaction baffled him. "I supposed that she would be glad to know the truth," he wrote. "I thought I could count on her cooperation in clearing up some of the mystery which surrounded her past. I hoped that we I [*sic*] might work out together the complete history of the case and make suitable plans for the protection of her associates in the future."

He wanted to save her from her carrier state. He wanted to teach her the proper hygiene methods in order to protect the families for whom she worked—and he expected her to be grateful for his help.

The sharp tines of Mary's carving fork said otherwise.

"I never felt more hopeless," said Soper after he left empty-handed.

✠

Soper may have felt hopeless, but he wasn't giving up. He felt certain that he had gathered enough epidemiological evidence to prove that Mary was spreading the killer disease.

At this point, however, the evidence that Mary Mallon caused typhoid wherever she worked was circumstantial. The fact that she happened to work at places where typhoid fever broke out did not prove that she caused the outbreaks. The outbreaks may have been a coincidence. The fact that Mary escaped the illness herself wasn't proof either. Nor was the fact that she left her employment soon after typhoid broke out.

But these facts—and her behavior—convinced Soper that Mary Mallon was "a menace to the public health." The circumstantial nature of the evidence did not deter him.

"As a matter of fact, I did not need the specimens in order to prove that Mary was a focus of typhoid germs," he said. "My epidemiological evidence had proved that."

Soper was wrong. He did need the specimens. As scientists and statisticians know, correlation does not imply causation. So far, he had only established a pattern that put Mary at the scene of the outbreaks. He needed the specimens to prove that Mary had caused the outbreaks.

But he did not have the authority to force Mary to comply. No sanitary engineer did. Only the powerful New York City Board of Health had that authority.

That raises this question: If Soper was certain that he had the epidemiological evidence, why didn't he report Mary to the health authorities right away? Perhaps, in order to convince the health officials that something needed to be done, he needed direct evidence—the specimens—that linked Mary to the typhoid cases. Or perhaps he didn't want to share the credit for discovering the first healthy carrier in the United States.

Whatever his reason—Soper doesn't say—he decided to act on his own. If he couldn't persuade Mary in the Bowens' kitchen, perhaps she'd be more willing to listen someplace else.

✢

Once more, George Soper worked like a detective. "I found that Mary was in the habit of going, when her work for the day was finished, to a rooming house on Third Avenue below Thirty-third Street," he recounted.

He doesn't state how he found this out. It is likely that as she left the kitchen of the Park Avenue house, he followed her for thirty-nine blocks, all the way to the rooming house. Perhaps he stood beneath the elevated train tracks that rose above Third Avenue and watched as she let herself inside.

This raised his suspicions about Mary. Soper snooped around the neighborhood, asking questions. He learned that an out-of-work policeman known as August Breihof lived on the top floor and that Mary often visited Breihof, bringing him dinner, most likely leftovers from the Park Avenue kitchen.

Soper didn't approve of Mary's visits. "She was spending the evenings with a disreputable-looking man who had a room on the top floor," Soper wrote. "His headquarters during the day was a saloon on the corner."

While Mary was at work, Soper befriended Breihof. Perhaps he bought Mary's friend a drink or two at the saloon. Perhaps he waited until Breihof had too much to drink. However it happened, Soper convinced Mary's friend to show him the room where he lived.

Soper followed Breihof to the top floor of the rooming house, where Breihof opened the door to his room. Soper was disgusted by what he saw. "I should not care to see another like it," he wrote. "It was a place of dirt and disorder."

We don't know much about August Breihof. New York City directories for the years 1903 to 1908 list his occupation as policeman. From census records, it seems that he was born in Manhattan in 1856, making him fifty-one years old when Soper met him.

From Soper, we learn that Breihof was out of work, lived in a run-down flat, and spent too much time drinking. His only friends in the world were Mary Mallon and a large motley dog. From Soper, we also learn that August Breihof had a heart condition.

Recent historians speculate that Mary must have loved Breihof, despite his faults. She brought him supper. She was fond of his dog. She overlooked the fact that he spent his days in a saloon and drank too much and didn't work.

Some claim that Mary lived with Breihof, although Soper states only that she spent her evenings with him. Others suggest that Mary may have paid his rent and given him drinking money.

From Soper's accounts, we know that Mary's friendship with Breihof and her fondness for his big dog disgusted Soper.

Soper doesn't speculate on how Mary Mallon could have cooked for Breihof yet not made him sick. It's possible that Breihof had recovered from typhoid at some point in his life and was naturally immune, just as Mary's former employer J. Coleman Drayton was.

Soper convinced Breihof to allow him to wait for Mary after work. We don't know what Soper said or did to convince Breihof. Perhaps Breihof was drunk. Perhaps Soper slipped him a few dollars. Perhaps Soper wasn't forthright about his intentions. However it happened, the two men set a meeting time, and Soper left.

This time Soper vowed to do better. He would be more patient with Mary. He would choose better words and speak more carefully. He would use as much tact and good judgment as he could muster. He would plan out what he'd say, and rehearse the words.

"[I wanted] to make sure she understood what I meant," said Soper, "and that I meant her no harm."

But he wouldn't face Mary Mallon alone. He would bring an associate.

Chapter Seven

IN WHICH EXTRAORDINARY AND ARBITRARY POWERS ARE AT WORK

At the appointed time, George Soper stood outside Breihof's door. He had brought along Bert Hoobler, a friend and associate who was also a medical doctor. The two men waited in the dimly lit hallway for Mary to return from work.

We don't know where Breihof was, if he was bellied up to the bar in his favorite corner saloon or cowering inside his room, knowing that he had betrayed Mary.

At last the rooming house door creaked opened and closed. Mary's thick-soled shoes could be heard on the stairs. She must have been tired after fourteen hours or more spent on her feet. She may have splurged on a ticket for a horse-drawn taxi or for the elevated train. Most likely, she walked the thirty-nine blocks home.

Mary rounded the last stairwell and, at the top, came face-to-face with the two men. She recognized Soper right away. "Mary was angry at the unexpected sight of me," he acknowledged later.

If Soper was nervous, he didn't say. He addressed Mary, using the words he had scripted.

"We explained our suspicions," recalled Soper. "We pointed out the need of examinations which might reveal the source of the infectious matter which Mary was, to a practical certainty, producing." Again, Soper requested samples of her urine, feces, and blood.

Mary ranted and swore. She'd never had typhoid fever, she told the two men. She was in perfect health and had no sign or symptom of any disease about her. She'd never made anyone sick.

Her rage escalated. She would not allow anybody to accuse her. She would not give them specimens. Typhoid fever was found everywhere in the city, she said. The instances that Soper cited could have come from anywhere and anyone, not from her.

Mary had a point. In 1907 the New York City Department of Health would report 4,476 cases, resulting in 740 deaths. Why should Mary be blamed when the disease was rampant throughout the city?

Mary insisted that she hadn't caused typhoid but had helped nurse the sick through their illness. She told Soper and Hoobler about the grateful employer—the wealthy Manhattan lawyer J. Coleman Drayton—who had given her a fifty-dollar bonus for helping him and his family throughout the illness. Wasn't that proof?

Mary probably didn't understand that she could be a healthy carrier. She probably didn't understand—or didn't accept—the scientific fact that tiny microscopic organisms invisible to the naked eye caused disease and that a person who looked and felt healthy might carry and spread germs.

We don't know why Mary didn't trust science and doctors. According to social research, a person's trust level is set by his or her mid-twenties. After your mid-twenties, your level of trust is unlikely to change. Furthermore, the more you distrust people, social researchers say, the less civil you're likely to act and behave toward others. Perhaps Mary's life experiences had taught her not to trust science and doctors or people in authority.

Although germ theory was widely accepted by

medical doctors and scientists, others contested the theory. For example, the famous Dr. Elizabeth Blackwell, the first woman to earn a medical degree in the United States—in 1849—rejected the germ theory of disease. She believed that disease was caused by immoral behavior, not a chance encounter with germs.

Other people held old-fashioned ideas that sickness and disease were caused by exposure to miasma, a foul-smelling poisonous mist or vapor that arose from garbage, filth, and the sewers. In other words, if something smelled bad, it could cause disease.

Mary Mallon wasn't all that different from many Americans today. Whereas the majority of Americans today—as high as 96 percent, according to a recent Gallup poll—trust their doctors, only 36 percent trust the information they get from scientists and the scientific community.

Fifty-one percent of Americans say they trust scientists and the scientific information a little bit. Six percent don't trust scientists and their facts at all. If Mary were alive today, she might be part of the 6 percent who don't trust science or, at best, part of the 51 percent who only partially trust science.

Mary also didn't trust George Soper and the New

York City Board of Health, which oversaw the Department of Health. The Board of Health was composed of medical doctors, the police commissioner, and other professionals. Some members were appointed by the city mayor; others were appointed by the governor.

By comparison, many Americans today—as many as 79 percent—don't trust their local government. They also don't trust government agencies such as their department of health.

Even today, there are people who adhere to old-fashioned—and sometimes wrong-headed—ideas about sickness and disease. For example, you can't catch a cold or the flu by not wearing a coat or having wet feet or sleeping in a drafty room. (You must come in contact with bacteria and viruses.) You should not starve a fever and feed a cold. (Both illnesses need the nutrients of a balanced diet to fight off infection.) Vitamin C will not cure the common cold (but it's an important antioxidant, a substance that repairs cells damaged by everyday activities). Garlic and onions will not ward off or cure the flu (but your breath may ward off friends and family if you eat them). The best way to avoid catching and spreading a contagious disease is to arm yourself with the correct medical information, get vaccinated, take the proper precautions, and practice good hygiene and sanitation habits.

As Mary raged in the hallway, Soper concluded that he would not reason with such an emotional and irrational woman. The two men retreated, escaping down the stairs. The whole while, Mary swore at them, throwing at them "a volley of imprecations."

"We were glad to close the interview and get down to the street," Soper recalled. "We agreed that it would be hopeless to try again."

Mary never spoke of the incident. We are left to imagine what transpired when she faced her friend Breihof, who had betrayed her.

✢

As George Soper fled the rooming house, he was convinced more than ever that Mary Mallon was an irrational woman.

Once again, he had explained the situation to her and spoken of her responsibility to protect others. He had pleaded in the interest of science and humanitarian considerations. But she was too emotional and irrational to understand. Therefore, he concluded, science and human life meant nothing to her.

✢

Over the coming days, Mary continued to cook for the Bownes. We don't know how many days, but the fact that Mary wasn't fired raises some questions: Did the Bownes know about Soper's suspicions? If so, why did they keep her on? Is it possible that the Bownes liked and trusted Mary and didn't believe she was a healthy carrier—the healthy carrier, in fact, who had likely infected their daughter?

At some point, someone—we don't know who—told Soper that Mary was going to quit her Park Avenue employment.

This alarmed him. If Mary quit, it would be difficult, if not impossible, to find her. Soper reasoned that a woman like Mary Mallon could not be allowed to roam free. His mind leaped to the great danger she presented to New York City. It was clearly a race against the clock. Lives were at stake.

The epidemic fighter hurried to the New York City Department of Health. He met with two members of the Board of Health: Dr. Thomas Darlington, commissioner of health, and Dr. Hermann Biggs, general medical officer of the Department of Health.

Behind closed doors, Soper painted a doomsday scenario of the cook spreading killer germs throughout the city. He created a persuasive story, using words that dehumanized Mary and turned her into a dangerous machine. He called Mary "a living culture tube" and "a chronic typhoid germ producer."

"I said she was a proved menace to the community," Soper explained later. "It was impossible to deal with her in a reasonable and peaceful way."

In order to protect the public from the deadly cook, Soper said, the health department had to take the cook into custody and conduct a bacteriological examination of her urine, feces, and blood.

Recalling Mary's strength and temper, Soper warned Biggs, "If the Department meant to examine her, it must be prepared to use force and plenty of it."

✣

Soper's recommendation to arrest Mary raises the question of her civil rights.

So far, the evidence against her was still circumstantial at best. She wasn't visibly ill; in fact, by outward appearances she looked healthy. She had committed no crime. She had violated no laws. She was a hard-working legal citizen. If Mary Mallon didn't agree to the examination, did the city have the right to take her into custody? To force her to submit to an examination? What about Mary's civil rights?

Our civil and legal protections are spelled out in twenty-seven amendments to the United States Constitution. The first ten amendments make up the Bill of Rights, which was ratified in 1791. The Bill of Rights was created to protect individual liberties.

The Fourth Amendment protects an individual's right to be secure in his or her person, house, papers, and effects against unreasonable searches and seizure. An authority must show "probable cause," or reasons, for any search or seizure. If the cause is warranted, a judge must issue a warrant that describes the place to be searched and the persons or things to be seized, unless an exception applies. Otherwise, generally speaking, an authority cannot force someone to give a blood sample or other body specimen without the victim's consent.

An individual suspected of a crime also has a right to due process, or fair treatment. Two amendments, the Fifth and Fourteenth Amendments, protect this right. The Fifth Amendment states that no person "shall be . . . deprived of life, liberty, or property without due process of law" through the judicial system.

The Fourteenth Amendment strengthens the protection of due process and further stipulates that "no state make or enforce any law which shall abridge the privileges of citizens of the United States." In other words, each and every citizen is guaranteed equal protection of the law.

But no individual's civil and legal rights are absolute—especially when it comes to the protection of the public's health. Today, state and local laws are based on federal laws and may vary. These laws require health-care providers to report certain infectious diseases to the local and state health departments and possibly the Centers for Disease Control and Prevention, or CDC for short, a federal agency located in Atlanta, Georgia.

There are nearly one hundred reportable diseases. When most people discover they might have an infectious disease, they usually comply and do what their doctor tells them. In those rare instances when an infectious person doesn't comply, public health officials can require that person to undergo an examination and treatment. Still, health officials must follow the law. They must respect a person's legal rights. That means public health officials must work within the law and with law enforcement officials and the court. They must treat people who suffer from disease fairly.

In 1907, however, the New York City Department of Health had a board of medical doctors that had "legislative, judicial, and executive powers." This gave the Board of Health absolute power: it could create laws, pass the laws it created, and enforce the laws it made. Moreover, its regulations on public health matters were final. No other person or body could review or reverse its decisions.

Years later, Dr. Biggs admitted that the power wielded by the New York City Board of Health was unique. "I do not think that any sanitary authorities anywhere have had granted to them such extraordinary and even arbitrary powers as rest in the hands of the Board of Health," Biggs told a group of health officials at an international conference.

But never before had the health department arrested someone who appeared healthy.

Biggs listened carefully to Soper. He agreed that Mary had to undergo an examination in order to protect the public's health. In doing so, Biggs relied on a provision of the Greater New York Charter. He believed that the charter gave the health department the right to take Mary into custody. Moreover, he believed that the charter made it the department's duty to do so. Provision 1169 of the charter stated:

> It shall be the duty of said board of health to aid the enforcement of, and so far as prac-

tical, to enforce all laws of this state, applicable in said district, to the preservation of human life, or to the care, promotion, or protection of health; and said board may exercise the authority given by said laws to enable it to discharge the duty hereby imposed. . . . The board of health shall use all reasonable means for ascertaining the existence and cause of disease or peril to life or health, and for averting the same, throughout the city.

Still, Biggs didn't want to use force. He wished to get the specimens peacefully, if possible. Perhaps a woman would have a better chance with Mary Mallon, he decided.

And Biggs knew just the woman for the job.

Chapter Eight

IN WHICH MARY FIGHTS LIKE A CAGED LION

No one at the health department told the tiny woman that Mary might be difficult. Not Hermann Biggs. Not George Soper. Not even her boss, Dr. Walter Bensel. They kept Mary's temper and temperament a secret.

"I learned afterward that Dr. Soper had reason to suspect that Mary might make trouble," Dr. Josephine Baker wrote in her autobiography. "But I knew nothing of that."

On Monday, March 18, 1907, Dr. Baker headed to the Bownes' townhouse at 688 Park Avenue, where Soper had first confronted Mary. Baker believed she was on a routine call to collect blood, feces, and urine.

No doubt the case felt personal to Baker. She had

lost her father to typhoid when she was sixteen. He had caught the disease from contaminated water. She knew firsthand the ravages of the disease and the effect it had had on her and her family.

As a result of her personal loss, she gave up a scholarship to Vassar College and attended medical school instead. She graduated from the Women's Medical College of the New York Infirmary in 1898.

In 1907 Baker was one of the few female physicians in New York City. Instead of having a private medical practice, she became a roving inspector for the health department. Her job took her deep into the Lower East Side's tenement district, where she worked closely with impoverished mothers and their children.

Though she came from a well-to-do family, Baker devoted her life to improving the health of the poor. She understood the connection between poverty and poor health: The poor didn't have the same access to adequate nutrition, safe and sanitary housing, and health care. These conditions increased the risk factors for contagious diseases.

By 1907, the city had initiated public water and public sewer projects, as well as street cleaning and regular garbage removal. The city had also passed the Tenement House Act in order to improve living conditions. The new law required tenements to provide fire escapes, better ventilation, and access to natural light.

These important improvements reduced the incidence of disease, but they did not address the reasons for poverty. Many people continued to live in dire conditions, especially in the Lower East Side, where large immigrant families and their boarders crowded into two- and three-room flats in over 80,000 tenement buildings.

As a medical examiner, Baker saw the effects of poverty firsthand. Even with the new law, the tenements were overcrowded and dirty. Families lacked healthful food and medical care. Some simply didn't have enough food.

Working mostly with immigrant families, Baker delivered babies and taught mothers how to care for their children. She worked to improve hygiene and sanitary conditions.

It was terribly hard work. "I climbed stair after stair, knocked on door after door, met drunk after drunk, filthy mother after filthy mother and dying baby after dying baby," Baker recalled. "It was the hardest physical labor I ever did in my life; just backache and perspiration and disgust and discouragement and aching feet day in and day out."

Baker was prejudiced when it came to Irish immigrants, whom she called "incredibly shiftless" and "wholly lacking in any ambition and dirty to an unbelievable degree." For this reason, she may have been surprised when she saw Mary Mallon in the Park Avenue kitchen. Mary did not fit Baker's low opinion of Irish immigrants, for there stood a clean, neat woman wearing a blue calico dress. She had a firm mouth and her hair was wound in a tight knot at the back of her head. Baker called Mary a "self-respecting" woman.

Mary's appearance may have encouraged Baker. Using as much tact as possible, she told Mary that she had come to collect urine and blood samples.

Mary set her jaw. "No," she said, and returned to her work.

"She said it in a way that left little room for persuasion or argument," wrote Baker.

Baker summed Mary up quickly. "Obviously, here was another case of the blind, panicky distrust of doctors and all their works which crops up so often among the uneducated," she said. Then she added, "And among the educated too, for that matter."

Later, Baker wrote that she felt like a failure when

she left Mary's kitchen without the specimens. She dreaded making the telephone call to Dr. Bensel telling him she hadn't collected them.

Baker may have felt like a failure, but others knew her as wiry, shrewd, and ingenious. More than likely, her resolve hardened, for this tiny woman—whose friends called her "Dr. Joe" and who wore man-tailored suits and shirts and stiff collars and ties so that her male colleagues didn't dismiss her or condescend to her because she was female—did not back down from a fight.

Ten years earlier, fresh out of medical school, Baker had slugged a drunken man who had thrown scalding water on his pregnant wife. "I doubled my fist and hit him," she said. "It was beautifully timed. . . . He toppled backward, struck about a third of the way down the rather long stair and slid to the bottom with a hideous crash."

She didn't know if she had killed him—and didn't care. "He was in the way and not fit to live anyhow and I had taken the first handy means of getting rid of him," wrote Baker. "I was not sorry."

But, she added, "I was not glad either—it had just been part of the exigencies of this particular job."

The man lay at the foot of the stairs, but he wasn't dead. Baker had knocked him out cold. On her way out of the building, she stepped over his body. He awoke in time to swear at her.

After making the difficult phone call about Mary Mallon to her superior, Baker awaited further instructions. Later that night, Bensel called her, telling her to wait at the corner of Park Avenue and Sixty-seventh Street at seven-thirty sharp the next morning. There, an ambulance and three policemen would be waiting for her.

"We were to go to this house, get the blood and urine specimens," said Baker, "and, if Mary resisted, we were to take her to the Willard Parker Hospital, by force if necessary."

Little did Baker know that she and Mary shared the same sort of strength and determination—and that Mary, too, didn't back down from a fight.

✠

That night it snowed lightly. The next morning, March 19, Baker waited with three policemen at the snow-covered corner, as Bensel had instructed. Soon a horse-drawn ambulance pulled up.

Baker stationed one police officer around the corner from the house and another in front of the house. The third officer accompanied her to the servants' back entrance. This way, she figured, all possible escape routes were blocked.

Escorted by the officer, she approached the kitchen door and knocked. To her shock, Mary had already spotted her and was armed and ready, holding "a long kitchen fork in her hand like a rapier." She lunged at Baker with the fork.

Caught off-guard—it seems that Soper didn't warn Baker about carving forks—Baker recoiled, falling backwards onto the officer.

This time it was Mary who bolted back through the kitchen.

Too late, Baker and the police officer scrambled to their feet. "By the time we got through the door," wrote Baker, "Mary had disappeared. . . . She had completely vanished."

Baker and the police officers searched the house from top to bottom, but they could not find Mary. They questioned the maids, but the maids denied seeing her.

The search party moved to the backyard. There, Baker spotted footprints in the snow. She followed the footprints to a tall fence. A chair had been propped next to the fence, and snow was knocked off the top of the fence. Someone had scaled it.

The police officers searched the neighbor's house, but found no sign of Mary. The servants were questioned. No one admitted seeing Mary or knew where she might be.

"It was utter defeat," said Baker.

She telephoned her supervisor, giving him the hard news about Mary's escape.

Dr. Bensel wasn't interested in excuses. "I expect you to get the specimens or to take Mary to the hospital," he told Baker, and hung up.

✠

Enlisting the help of two more policemen, Baker searched for two more hours. "We went through every closet and nook and cranny in those two houses," she said.

Discouraged, Baker called it quits. As she started out the front door and down the stairs, Baker worried about how she would face her boss.

Baker and the policemen stood on the sidewalk. One of the policemen tapped her arm and pointed to several ashcans piled in front of a door beneath the stoop. A tiny fold of blue calico was stuck in the door. The exact calico of the dress Mary was wearing.

Euphoric, Baker realized that the maids had helped hide Mary. She admired the way the servants had stuck together, calling it "evidence of class solidarity." As distressed as she was, Baker said, she "liked that loyalty."

Together, she and the policemen pulled away the ashcans and pried open the door. "She came out fighting and swearing," wrote Baker, "both of which she could do with appalling efficiency and vigor."

Once more, she tried to reason with Mary: "I made another effort to talk to her sensibly."

But talk proved futile. Mary was convinced that the Board of Health was persecuting her when she had done nothing wrong and never had typhoid fever. "She was maniacal in her integrity," wrote Baker. "There was nothing I could do but take her with us."

And so Baker did. She ordered the policemen to force Mary into the ambulance.

Mary kicked and screamed and swore and fought for her life. It took four policemen to lift her into the vehicle. Baker climbed in behind them. To keep Mary from escaping, the tiny doctor sat on her chest, pinning her to the floor of the ambulance.

Though today medical professionals are trained to avoid language that dehumanizes their patients, Baker wrote, "It was like being in a cage with an angry lion."

Later, Baker would tell a reporter, "The hardest dollars I ever earned were those I got as a $100-a-month Health Department employee when I was sent to get Mary Mallon."

Chapter Nine

IN WHICH MARY'S BAD BEHAVIOR LEADS TO HER DOOM

Mary had met her match. In the ambulance, she screamed and kicked and swore as the horses galloped their way downtown to Willard Parker Hospital. The quarantine hospital was located along the East River on East Sixteenth Street and Second Avenue, on the Lower East Side.

There, Mary was sequestered in an outside isolation ward. Everything in the room was white: white walls, white ceiling, white floors. It had a white bed and a small white sink. A small closet held a white toilet, which Mary would have no choice but to use.

Mary wore a white bathrobe. It was all she had to wear, since the hospital attendants had confiscated her clothing, just as if she were a prisoner. She was not allowed to use the telephone or write a letter to contact anyone, not even Breihof.

For a fiercely independent woman such as Mary, who had always taken care of herself, Willard Parker Hospital was a great insult. The hospital was a teaching facility where medical students studied such contagious diseases as measles, smallpox, cholera, typhus, yellow fever, tuberculosis, and typhoid. Its patients, who obviously suffered from these diseases, came from the poorest tenement house districts in New York City.

Mary had committed no crime, yet here she was, kidnapped, surrounded by sick people, cut off from the outside world, and forced to submit to medical tests. She had no idea how long the hospital intended to hold her. She was clearly frightened.

Her imprisonment was necessary, Soper explained, because the health department considered her "a dangerous and unreliable person who might try to escape if given a chance."

Baker also felt no pity for the woman. "If Mary had let me have the specimens I was sent to get, she might have been a free woman all of her life," said Baker. "It was her own bad behavior that inevitably led to her doom."

When Mary couldn't hold out any longer and used

the toilet, attendants collected the urine and stool specimens and sent them to the health department's laboratory. Her blood was taken too, without her consent and without a court order.

Mary's specimens were sent to the laboratory for analysis. They were given to bacteriologists, who examined them, looking for typhoid bacteria.

George Soper and health department authorities awaited the laboratory results.

✠

In the laboratory, bacteriologists isolated the bacteria they found in Mary's samples. They amplified the bacteria—grew it—in small flat dishes called petri dishes. Then they placed the bacteria between glass slides and examined the slides under a microscope, looking for typhoid germs.

The intestinal tract is a complex bacterial ecosystem. The large intestine's job is to squeeze every ounce of liquid, salt, and nutrients from the food we eat and drink. The leftover is expelled from our bodies as feces.

To do the work it needs to do, the large intestine is lined with billions of microbes—helpful bacteria—that help our bodies digest the things we eat and drink. Human excrement consists of 75 percent water and 25 percent solid matter. If you're healthy, 30 percent of the solid matter is dead bacteria that helped you digest.

Your kidneys create urine, which passes into your bladder. In your bladder, the urine is sterile and contains no bacteria unless you're sick.

✠

The bacteriologists had found no bacteria in Mary's urine. But they found that the bacteria voided in her feces were a pure culture of the deadly typhoid bacilli. This meant there was a good chance that the germs had colonized in her gall bladder.

The bacteriologists sent their report to Dr. William Hallock Park, director of the bacteriological laboratory.

Park read the report. He telephoned Soper to relay the news. Despite Mary Mallon's rosy cheeks, good teeth, crisp blue eyes, fair skin, and apparent good health, she was a carrier of typhoid fever.

Soper was ecstatic about the findings. "The cook was virtually a living culture tube," he said, just as he had suspected.

Although Mary denied ever having typhoid fever, the laboratory results proved that she had suffered from the disease at some point in her life.

Was Mary lying? Not necessarily. She may have been too young to remember or the illness may have been so slight that it felt like the flu. Perhaps nobody—not even Mary—recognized the symptoms as the deadly typhoid disease.

Admittedly, it was an extraordinary predicament. When a disease strikes, a battle begins between the germs and the victim's immune system. In most typhoid cases—97 percent of the time—either the typhoid germs win and the victim dies, or the victim's immune system wins and the typhoid germs die.

In a small number of cases—roughly 3 percent—the victim recovers but continues to harbor the deadly bacteria for several months.

In an even smaller number of cases—about 1 percent or less—the disease results in a draw. Neither the germs nor the immune system wins. The victim recovers but carries the typhoid germs for life.

In these cases, the typhoid bacteria have colonized in the gallbladder. Once the initial illness passes, the victim has no symptoms. For all intents and purposes, these victims go about their lives, never suspecting that they are as sick as someone who has the disease and that they are shedding the germs, making others sick.

This is what happened in Mary's case. But her circumstances were even more extraordinary because it seems that her immune system fought off the disease so well that no one—not even Mary—knew that she was sick in the first place.

For George Soper, this discovery was a major breakthrough. "We have here, in my judgment, a case of a chronic typhoid germ distributor," said Soper. "Or, as the Germans say, a '*Typhusbazillenträgerin.*'"

At last, he hoped, Mary Mallon would listen to reason—and to a big idea that he had.

✠

George Soper paid her a visit in the hospital. "Mary," he said, "I've come to talk with you and see if between us we cannot get you out of here."

By now, according to newspaper accounts, Mary had spent several days at Willard Parker. Scolding her as if she were a child who had disobeyed her parents, Soper warned Mary that her hospital stay depended upon her behavior. "When I have asked you to help me before, you have refused," he said, "and when others have asked you, you have refused them also."

Like Dr. Baker, George Soper believed that Mary had no one to blame but herself. "You would not be where you are now if you had not been so obstinate," he told her. "So throw off your wrong-headed idea and be reasonable."

As he spoke, Soper noticed that Mary glared at him. By now she had had plenty of time to brood. Her mood did not improve with Soper's visit and the way he addressed her.

We don't know if Mary's growing anger made him uncomfortable. Perhaps he felt safe, knowing that hospital attendants were close by and that she didn't have a carving fork. He tried to calm her, saying, "Nobody wants to harm you."

Yet nothing Soper said could make Mary trust him. Why should she place her trust in this man? If no one wanted to harm her, why had she been kidnapped, as she later described in a letter? Why was she locked in a hospital room with her freedom and dignity robbed from her?

Convinced that he might persuade her to listen, Soper launched into another carefully rehearsed speech. "You say you have never caused a case of typhoid," he said, "but I know you have done so. Nobody thinks you have done it purposely. But you have done it just the same. Many people have been made sick and have suffered a great deal; some have died. You refused to give specimens which would help to clear up the trouble. So you were arrested and brought here and the specimens taken in spite of your resistance. They proved what I charged. Now you must surely see how mistaken you were. Don't you acknowledge it?"

Soper pressed further. "I'll tell you how you do it," he said. "When you go to the toilet, the germs within your body get upon your fingers and when you handle food in cooking they get on the food. People who eat this food swallow the germs and get sick. If you would wash your hands after leaving the toilet and before cooking, there might be no trouble. You don't keep your hands clean enough."

He must have added insult to injury, telling Mary that she had dirty habits, that she didn't wash her hands.

Soper noted that her anger continued to grow as he explained that the germs were growing inside her gallbladder. He tried to assure Mary, telling her that surgeons could fix her and her problem. If she would be reasonable and see things his way, he could help her become better and new and clean again.

"The best way to get rid of [the germs] is to get rid of the gallbladder," Soper told her. "You don't need a gallbladder any more than you need an appendix. There are many people living without them."

It's true. Your gallbladder is a small organ, about the size of a pear. It's located in the upper right quadrant of your abdomen, just below your liver. Its main function is to store the bile produced by your liver. After you eat, the bile moves into your small intestine to help your body break down the fats you consumed. As important as this function is, you can live without a gallbladder. Your body will adjust and store the excess bile in your bile ducts.

But Mary was frightened. At last she knew what the health department wanted. They wanted to perform surgery on her. They wanted her gallbladder. Later, Mary would reveal her fear that the health department wanted her out of the way and that they were trying to murder her.

Mary's fear wasn't baseless. Stories of murderers and grave robbers who sold bodies to medical doctors for anatomic study and dissection are found in Irish history and folk history. Two of the most famous serial murderers, William Burke and William Hare, were Irish immigrants who sold bodies to the Edinburgh Medical School in Scotland in 1828. One of the murderers—William Burke—was born in County Tyrone, Ireland, where Mary had lived. No doubt she had heard the stories.

As Soper talked, Mary remained quiet. Her reticence encouraged him to push on. He would help her, he said. "If you will answer my questions, I will do everything I possibly can to get you out," he promised.

Then Soper revealed his motive for helping her. "I will do more than you think," he said. "I will write a book about your case. I will not mention your real name; I will carefully hide your identity. I will guarantee that you will get all the profits."

Years later, Soper explained his offer. "The information would help many," he said. "It could not possibly hurt her. It might prove helpful in explaining her case. As matters stood, nobody accused her of deliberately intending any harm. If possible, she was to be freed from her disease-producing capacity."

Soper didn't mention the fame that Mary's cooperation would bring him. He would make history as the first to identify a healthy carrier in the United States.

Mary stood, pulling her white bathrobe tightly around her. Did this raise his hopes? Was she prepared to seal the deal with a handshake?

Without uttering a word, Mary crossed the room, opened the door to the toilet, and stepped inside. The door slammed behind her.

Mary had made her point. "There was no need of my waiting," Soper said. "It was apparent that Mary did not intend to speak to me. So I left the place."

The engineer had lost yet another battle with the cook.

Chapter Ten

IN WHICH THERE'S SOME NAME-CALLING

On April 2, about two weeks after her arrest, Mary's story was published in the *New York American* newspaper. Nobody knows who leaked Mary's story to the press. The newspaper simply said that the informant was a "well-known member of the Board of Health."

No doubt the newsboys who hawked newspapers on the city streets shouted the headline "HUMAN TYPHOID GERM." No doubt readers who liked a good scare story bought the newspaper.

The millionaire publisher William Randolph Hearst owned the *New York American,* and if anyone knew how to sell newspapers, he did. In 1907 his popular morning newspaper had a daily circulation of 300,000, second only to Joseph Pulitzer's *New York World,* with its circulation of 313,000.

Both publishers had discovered that the more sensational the news stories, the more overly dramatized, the more frightening and inflammatory, the more newspapers they sold. This popular style of journalism became known as "yellow journalism" in the 1890s. The phrase stuck.

Soon "yellow journalism" referred to a style of reporting that exaggerated and distorted the news and even altered the facts to fit the story.

Today the term is still used to describe journalism that sensationalizes or is unprofessional or unethical. Such stories appear in certain popular tabloids and online publications but do not usually appear in reputable newspapers.

William Randolph Hearst's *New York American* was the first to report the story of the imprisoned Irish cook. Like George Soper, the reporter dehumanized Mary, making her into a frightening half human, half machine. He called her a "human typhoid germ," a "human culture tube," a "human fever factory," and a "human vehicle."

"She is practically a human vehicle for typhoid fever germs," said the reporter. "There are millions of them in her system, and the physicians and surgeons are baffled in their attempts to rid the woman of the infinitesimal creatures that are enemies of mankind."

The reporter tried to wrangle the cook's name out of hospital officials, but the officials wouldn't reveal her identity. They dubbed her "Mary Ilverson," an Irish girl, and said she was housed in Bellevue Hospital, not Willard Parker.

In the news story, the reporter exaggerated Mary's circumstances. He referred to her not as a patient, but as a "prisoner" whose "case [was] hedged about with more safeguards against publicity and attended by more mysterious circumstances than any which has been recorded in Bellevue Hospital for years." He also claimed that the attendants guarded Mary because "she constantly makes attempts to escape."

✠

Today, federal law provides statutes that guard medical privacy. The most common law is the Health Insurance Portability and Accountability Act, known as the HIPAA Privacy Rule.

The Privacy Rule protects most health records from disclosure. For example, health officials cannot disclose an adult's private medical information without the patient's permission—not even to family members. Children have special privacy rights too, although these rights vary from state to state. But the law does permit health-care providers—a doctor, for example—to disclose information about reportable diseases to public health officials.

In 1907 no law protected Mary's privacy or health records. This begs the question: Why did health officials keep her case a secret? Was the New York City Department of Health trying to protect Mary Mallon? Or was the department trying to protect itself?

In a newspaper article, Dr. Walter Bensel explained the need to quarantine the cook. "This woman is a great menace to health, a danger to the community, and she has been made a prisoner on that account," he said. "In her wake are many cases of typhoid fever, she having unwittingly disseminated—or, as we might say, sprinkled—germs in various households."

The newspaper credited George Soper with finding the cook who had caused "thirty-eight persons for whom she worked to contract typhoid fever." In actuality, Soper counted twenty-four cases, including the Bowen daughter who had died.

✢

At the time health department officials took Mary Mallon into custody, typhoid fever was a national crisis, causing 28,971 deaths across the country in 1907 alone.

Many Americans believed that the government had a responsibility to protect them from infectious diseases such as typhoid—even if it meant that individuals such as Mary Mallon lost their freedom.

Quarantine is nothing new. For thousands of years, sick people have been quarantined. In the Old Testament book of Leviticus 13:1–46, for example, rules are given for the treatment of those with skin diseases and for the isolation of lepers. Known as Hansen's disease today, leprosy is an infection caused by bacteria. The disease causes skin sores and nerve damage, and muscle weakness that worsens over time. Today, the disease is extremely rare. Cases must be reported to health authorities, but quarantine is usually not necessary. The disease is easily treated with antibiotics.

For the most part, the discoveries of antibiotics and immunizations have made quarantine and quarantine hospitals a practice of the past for many of the most contagious diseases that were once feared. Under certain conditions, however, certain diseases may require special care and even quarantine. According to the

Communicable Disease Center (CDC), these diseases include cholera, diphtheria, infectious tuberculosis, plague, smallpox, severe acute respiratory syndrome (SARS), and viral hemorrhagic fevers such as yellow fever and ebola.

Most Americans today believe the government has a responsibility to protect them from infectious diseases. Public health laws require that certain communicable diseases must be reported, victims must be treated, and if necessary, victims must be isolated while they are treated. Health officials strive to respect a victim's autonomy, liberty, and privacy, but these rights are not absolute when the public's health and safety are threatened.

Just as many people today feel anxious about the spread of germs, so did those living in Mary's time. Despite the widespread acceptance of germ theory, many didn't understand how germs spread or that germs don't discriminate. Some people chose not to believe medical science. Instead, out of ignorance or fear, they clung to old-fashioned and completely wrong ideas. For example, many upper- and middle-class people worried about catching germs from the lower classes.

In 1897 Mrs. Plunkett, the author of a popular household hygienc book, warned, "The zephyrs will come along and pick up the disease germs and bear them onward, distributing them to whomever it meets, whether he be a millionaire or a shillingaire . . ."

Employers feared that their very own servants—a cook such as "Mary Ilverson"—might bring germs into their family.

Still, health department officials were in a quandary over Mary. The provisions of the Greater New York Charter were written in 1897, before health officials understood the concept of a healthy carrier. Provision 1170 stated:

> Said board [of health] may remove or cause to be removed to [a] proper place to be by it designated, any person sick with any contagious, pestilential or infectious disease; shall have exclusive charge and control of the hospitals for the treatment of such cases.

The city code referred only to people who were noticeably sick. Mary was not sick. No one could look at Mary and say that she had a contagious, pestilential, or infectious disease. Everyone who saw her noted her good health.

The health department had never quarantined a healthy person. Did it have the right to quarantine

Mary, a woman who *seemed* to make others sick while she remained healthy?

Health officials told the *New York American* reporter that they were appealing to eminent lawyers to determine their course of action.

Whether the officials sought legal counsel, we don't know. Whether they followed the advice of legal counsel, we don't know. No existing record shows that they did.

But we do know this: soon after the *New York American* reporter broke the story, health department officials acted quickly and quietly.

Without a lawyer, a court hearing, or a jury trial, Mary Mallon was packed off to Riverside Hospital, a quarantine facility where escape would be impossible.

The Riverside Hospital complex was located on North Brother Island, a thirteen-acre island in the middle of the East River, between Queens and the Bronx. The island was just a few hundred yards from shore, but strong river currents made it too dangerous to swim to shore or even to navigate a small boat.

There, health department officials hoped, Mary would learn to keep her germs to herself.

Chapter Eleven

IN WHICH MARY IS BANISHED LIKE A LEPER

At Sixteenth Street, hospital attendants escorted Mary onto a special steamer reserved for patients. The steamer carried her up the East River, and she arrived on North Brother Island frightened and angry and more resistant than ever.

The island had once been an uninhabited bit of land. Over the years, the city filled in the sandy, marshy ground and built a strong seawall to buffer the breakers. Its ten acres were transformed into thirteen.

In 1885 Riverside Hospital was moved from Blackwell's Island (now Roosevelt Island) to North Brother Island. The island became a temporary treatment and quarantine center for measles, smallpox, tuberculosis, scarlet fever, and typhus fever (not to be confused with typhoid fever) patients. Hospital patients came from the city's tenements.

In 1897 a police reporter named Jacob Riis described the island as a "garden spot," saying, "Today, where once was a waste of sand, are broad and shaded lawns; winding, well-kept walks, trees, shrubs and flowers; handsome, substantial buildings and hospital pavilions or wards." But, he added, "it can hardly be said that people are anxious to reside there."

Isolated from the other patients, Mary was given a small bungalow that sat on the riverbank. The cottage had a living room, a kitchen, and a bathroom, as well as such modern conveniences as gas, indoor plumbing, and electricity. She had a small fox terrier for company. Her identity was withheld. Health department reports referred to Mary simply as "a woman who had served as a cook."

From her cottage windows Mary could watch a ferryboat glide past. She could see gas tanks on the distant Bronx shore. At night she could hear the East River lap against the rocks.

✠

By the time Mary arrived on North Brother Island, the emotional stress of her arrest and quarantine had taken its toll.

"When I first came here I was so nervous and

almost prostrated with grief and trouble," she later wrote in a letter addressed to the editor of the *New York American*. "My eyes began to twitch and the left eyelid became paralyzed and would not move." The letter was never published.

For six months Mary couldn't close her left eyelid. According to her, no eye specialist examined her, even though one routinely visited other patients.

The twitching may have been caused by fatigue or stress or even a benign tumor that later went away on its own. And Mary's inability to close her eyelid could have been caused by an underlying medical condition, a psychological syndrome, or even a reaction to drugs.

Mary asked for an eye cover but was not given one. During the day she cupped her eye shut with her hand. At night she tied a bandage around her head to keep her eye closed.

Her eye eventually improved. In her letter to the *New York American,* she wrote, "However, my eye got better thanks to the Almighty God." Whatever Mary was about to say next, she must have changed her mind. She crossed out "& no thanks" and ended the sentence.

Two or three times a week, attendants collected fecal, urine, and blood specimens. Sometimes the results were positive; other times they were negative. This indicates that Mary was an intermittent carrier of typhoid fever.

The health department tried experimental drugs on her. Doctors prescribed Urotropin, a pharmaceutical drug made from a combination of ammonia and formaldehyde.

"I took the urotropin for about three months all told," said Mary. "If I should have continued, it would certainly have killed me for it was very severe. Everyone knows whoever is acquainted in any kind of medicine [*sic*] that it is used for *kidney* trouble."

The drug known as Urotropin was not effective on typhoid germs living in the gallbladder. The medication was administered to eliminate typhoid germs from the urine of patients who had recovered from typhoid, not for patients such as Mary.

Another doctor gave her some pills (she doesn't say what kind), a saline mixture called an "anti-autotox," and brewer's yeast. It was believed that these medicines and remedies would disinfect Mary's gastrointestinal canal. One doctor called anti-autotox "a proved measure" and said that "combined with colonic irrigation, treatment is most efficacious." It was not.

Such medical experimentation was fraught with danger, something that George Soper acknowledged.

"Anything that will kill the bacilli will apparently kill the individual who is the locus, as we say, for those bacilli," he said.

But to Soper, a typhoid epidemic had to be prevented at any cost. "The danger from the typhoid carrier must be stamped out," he told the *New York Times.* "Until it is stamped out, typhoid will still be with us."

The health department officials frightened Mary, for it seemed that no doctors could agree on where the problem lay or how to cure her.

"I'm a little afraid of the people and I have a good right," Mary admitted in her letter. "When I came to the Department, they said they [the germs] were in my intestinal tract. Later another said they were in the muscles of my bowels, and latterly, they thought of the gallbladder."

To Mary, it seemed as though her fear had been realized: the doctors had quarantined her for the purpose of medical research.

✠

The summer of 1907 ended. Mary turned thirty-eight in September. Christmas came and went. So did New Year's, and it was now 1908. The hospital permitted visitors two days a week, but the ferry stopped running during the winter months.

Later, reporters described Mary's life on the island, claiming that she lived in total isolation, shunned by the nurses and other attendants. "A keeper, three times a day, brings food to her door and then flees as if from a pestilence," wrote the *New York American*.

"They do not dread leprosy, smallpox, scarlet fever, and a score of other diseases," wrote another newspaper, the *New York Call*. "But they avoided the disseminator of typhoid germs and left her entirely to herself."

This wasn't entirely true. By now, Mary had made a close friend, a twenty-three-year-old registered nurse named Adelaide Jane Offspring. The two women were often seen together, walking the paths on the island. Offspring later wrote that Mary was permitted to have visitors.

Mary looked for ways to keep busy. "Often I help nurse the other patients on the Island and often the children will have no one else take care of them when they are very sick," she later told a *New York World* reporter.

And, of course, she had her small dog for company.

Mary continued to lobby for her release. "I never had typhoid in my life and have always been healthy," she told a *New York American* reporter in 1909. "Why should I be banished like a leper and compelled to live in solitary confinement with only a dog for a companion?"

After ten months hospital officials considered discharging her. The resident physician asked her where she would live if she were discharged.

"Naturally, I said New York," Mary wrote. After all, New York City had been her home for twenty-four years, ever since she had emigrated from Ireland.

But New York City Department of Health officials didn't want the responsibility. "So there was a stop put to my getting out of here," said Mary.

When the supervising nurse heard that Mary's release was refused, she told Mary to write to the officials, saying that if she were released, she would go to Connecticut to live with her sister. That would make her Connecticut's problem, not New York's.

But Mary wouldn't lie. "Well, I have no sister in Connecticut or in any other state in the US," she told the nurse, who then called her "a hopeless case."

Mary never said why she didn't consider returning to Ireland. Perhaps she couldn't afford passage. Perhaps she had no family left in Ireland. Perhaps she had a good reason to leave Ireland and never return.

More than likely, as a naturalized citizen of the United States, Mary knew that she had the right to stay in America. She was determined to fight her case and clear her name.

"I have been told that all I had to do was to apply to Dr. Darlington and promise to leave the State and live under another name and I could have my freedom," Mary told a *New York World* reporter. "But this I will not do. I will be either cleared or die where I now am."

✠

A year passed. The whole time, Mary remained determined to win her freedom. In July 1908 she arranged for her urine and feces to be analyzed by a private laboratory in Manhattan. Her friend August Breihof served as courier.

On visitation day Breihof rode the ferry across the river, donned the required long gown and high rubber overshoes at the dock, made his way to Mary's cottage, collected her specimens, and then took the ferry back to Sixteenth Street. He delivered the specimens to Ferguson Laboratories at 121 West Forty-second Street.

Over the next nine months Breihof delivered at

least ten specimens, taking a brief hiatus over the winter months when the ferry didn't run.

Each time, the report came back "This specimen gives negative results for typhoid." Not one specimen showed evidence of typhoid germs. Ironically, during these same weeks, Mary's specimens tested positive eight times in the New York City Department of Health laboratory.

But the Ferguson Laboratories results bolstered Mary's hopes. They confirmed what she had been saying all along: that she didn't have typhoid and had never suffered from the disease. The results reinforced her distrust in the city health department.

Why did the results contradict each other? It's possible that the specimens that reached the Ferguson Laboratories weren't fresh. (After all, Breihof was the deliveryman.) It's also possible that Ferguson technicians were careless or inefficient, thus tainting the results. And, as it's been noted, Mary was an intermittent carrier. Perhaps some weeks the typhoid germs just didn't show up.

It's also possible that Mary's worst fears were true: that the city had kidnapped her and quarantined her in order to conduct experimental medical research.

✢

Urged by Mary, August Breihof approached Dr. Thomas Darlington, the commissioner of health at the time of Mary's arrest, asking when Mary would be discharged.

Darlington didn't want to take responsibility for her release. "I cannot let her go myself."

He told Breihof that the decision rested with another Board of Health doctor, William Studdiford, who also didn't want the responsibility. He told Breihof that given the number of people Mary had infected, he couldn't release her. But he had an idea. Perhaps Breihof could convince Mary to agree to surgery to remove her gallbladder. He promised Breihof that the best surgeon in town would perform the operation—or "do the cutting," as Mary called it.

Breihof relayed this message to Mary, but she wouldn't budge. "No knife will be put on me," said Mary. "I've nothing the matter with my gallbladder."

In her letter, Mary explained that she could not trust doctors to cut her open when they couldn't even make up their minds about how to treat the germs they claimed were inside her.

More wary than ever, Mary worried that the doctors would etherize her and perform surgery just to experiment—or worse. "The Health Department just wants to use that way of murdering me," she said.

The hospital staff couldn't understand her reluctance. "Would it not be better for you to have it done than remain here?" asked a supervising nurse.

But Mary was adamant.

Mary was no physician, but her instincts were right. Even today, surgery is never without risk, and surgery was much more dangerous in 1908. There was a good chance she might not survive. If the operation didn't kill her, an infection might. Antibiotics would not be discovered for another thirty-four years.

Furthermore, even if she survived the gallbladder removal, her condition might stay the same, for the typhoid bacilli can also be found in the ileum, spleen, and bone marrow.

But George Soper didn't understand Mary's refusal. To him, it was just a gallbladder. "I understand that the gall bladder can be removed," he said. "Apparently, human beings can get along without it."

✠

While Mary was confined on North Brother Island, George Soper was making a name for himself. He traveled the country speaking about his great discovery.

In April 1907, one month after Mary's arrest, Soper

delivered a paper called "The Work of a Chronic Typhoid Germ Distributor" before the Biological Society of Washington, D.C. He never mentioned Mary's name. He detailed his work and his discovery of the deadly cook.

He published the same paper in the *Journal of the American Medical Association* during Mary's first month on North Brother Island. The paper and its discussion were published again in a journal called *Science* later that same year.

Dr. William Hallock Park was also speaking and writing about Mary, without revealing her last name. In June 1908 Dr. Park presented a paper called "Typhoid Bacilli Carriers" before a session at the American Medical Association. Three months later, the paper was published in the *Journal of the American Medical Association*.

At the AMA session, Park addressed the question of the city's right to quarantine the cook. "The case of this woman brings up many interesting problems," he said. "Has the city a right to deprive her of her liberty for perhaps her whole life? The alternative is to turn loose on the public a woman who is known to have infected at least twenty-eight persons." (Park was wrong; at this date, twenty-four, not twenty-eight, cases had been attributed to Mary.)

Park noted that Mary was not the only healthy carrier in New York City. Other seemingly healthy people also shed typhoid bacilli in their feces, yet he considered it impractical to quarantine each and every healthy carrier—"except as in the case of the cook already described." He didn't explain why Mary was the exception.

In the discussion that followed Park's lecture, another physician referred to the cook as "typhoid Mary." The name stuck. Newspapers, doctors, health officials, and the public began referring to Mary as "Typhoid Mary," a term that would come to mean a polluted or troublemaking woman who should be avoided.

For two years and three months, as Soper and Park delivered their lectures and published their papers, as they gained fame and notoriety within medical circles, Mary waited for the day when she could clear her name and win her release.

And then, one warm Sunday morning in June 1909, Mary Mallon opened the Sunday magazine section of the *New York American* and saw her full name and likeness splashed across two lurid pages.

Chapter Twelve

IN WHICH MARY MALLON HAS HER DAY IN COURT

"Typhoid Mary" Most Harmless and Yet the Most Dangerous Woman in America

The Extraordinary Predicament of Mary Mallon, a Prisoner on New York's Quarantine Hospital Island, Not Because She Is Sick, but Because She Breeds Typhoid Fever Germs and Scatters Them Wherever She Goes.

Mary stared at the pages. A large illustration depicted her wearing an apron and cracking skull-like typhoid bacilli into a frying pan. A photograph showed her lying in a hospital bed. Another showed her sitting in an outdoor pavilion with other patients. Across the banner headline marched the silhouettes of her victims.

One of William Randolph Hearst's reporters had broken the story. For the first time, Mary Mallon's full identity was revealed in the *New York American*. The Sunday-morning edition boasted a circulation of nearly 800,000. This meant that nearly 800,000 people—or more—knew Mary's name.

The double-page spread included the paper that George Soper had presented before the Biological Society of Washington D.C., but the *New York American* retitled it "The Extraordinary Trail of Death and Disease Left by Mary Mallon."

Dr. William Hallock Park wrote an accompanying untitled article in which he said, "Every effort has been made to cure the unfortunate woman, but so far without success." He added that it was "the plain duty of the health authorities to safeguard the public from such a menace." He predicted that Mary would be a prisoner for a very long time, possibly for life.

The reporter agreed. "It is probable that Mary Mallon is a prisoner for life," he wrote in the opening paragraph. Then, more sympathetically, he added, "And yet she has committed no crime, has never been accused of an immoral or wicked act, and has never been a prisoner in any court, nor has she been sentenced to imprisonment by any judge."

In Mary's letter to the editor of the *New York Amer-*

ican she revealed her resentment for the way she was treated: "I have been in fact a peep show for everybody. Even the interns had to come to see me and ask about the facts already known to the whole wide world. The tuberculosis men would say, 'There she is, the kidnapped woman.'"

She also revealed her bitter resentment for the way such men as Soper and Park were talking about her. "I wonder how the said Dr. William H. Park would like to be insulted and put in the *Journal* [newspaper] and call him or his wife Typhoid William Park."

Her letter was never published.

✠

One of the *New York American* readers was a thirty-four-year-old attorney named George Francis O'Neill. He called the circumstances that led to her imprisonment "absurd." Aghast at the clear violation of her civil rights, he offered to represent Mary Mallon.

To this day, no one knows exactly how she paid for George O'Neill's legal services. There is no evidence that he offered them for free.

Some believe that publisher William Randolph Hearst himself paid the attorney. Hearst was known as an advocate for the workingman and the underdog. His sensational newspaper often railed against social injustice. Plus, paying Mary's legal fees would be a good way to get the exclusive rights to her story. This would not be considered ethical today.

But the *New York American* itself credited several wealthy New Yorkers with paying Mary's legal fees. "[They] were moved by pity for the lone woman who has not a relative or a friend to whom she can turn," wrote the reporter.

George Francis O'Neill intended to give Mary Mallon her day in court, a right protected by the Sixth Amendment. She had the right to an attorney. She had the right to a speedy trial and an impartial jury. She had the right to be confronted with the witnesses against her. She had the right to obtain her own witnesses. These rights are part of the due process rights that are protected in the Fifth Amendment.

But first O'Neill had to force the health department to show in court why Mary was imprisoned. He headed to the New York State Supreme Court and filed a legal complaint known as a writ of habeas corpus, which requires a prison official to show why a prisoner is held.

At long last, Mary Mallon would have her day in court.

✠

Nine days after the story broke, more than two years and four months after an ambulance had carted Mary to Willard Parker Hospital, she boarded the hospital ferry that carried her to Sixteenth Street in Manhattan.

With her attorney, she headed to the New York Supreme Court at 52 Chambers Street in lower Manhattan. In her dress pocket she carried folded pages torn from the Sunday-morning *New York American*.

The courtroom reporters were impressed with Mary Mallon's appearance and good health. "No stranger who saw Mary yesterday would have suspected the danger the Health Board alleges it finds in this young woman," wrote a *New York American* reporter. "She has a clear, healthy complexion, regular features, bright eyes and white teeth. She looks to be in robust health."

Another reporter described Mary appearing "as rosy as you please." He remarked on her strength, saying that she looked "as though she could make as valid resistance as she did then [when she was arrested]."

Reporters also used language that connoted a witch or a sorceress. They described Mary as a woman who had "strange power" and who "possessed the power" to infect others. She was "one of the few freaks of the kind" who "made all ill who came in contact with her." An illustration showed an aproned Mary as a deadly cook, stirring a boiling pot. Skulls rose from the steam.

✠

The proceedings began. George Francis O'Neill stood before Justices Mitchell Erlanger and Leonard Giegerich. He claimed that no law justified Mary's arrest and imprisonment. Futhermore, O'Neill argued that her right to due process had been abridged. The health department had had no right to arrest Mary, lock her in a hospital room, and then take specimens without her consent.

Since Mary had no visible signs of illness, O'Neill argued, the health department "had a right to examine [Mary] first and then take [her], not take [her] and then examine [her]."

At last, Mary had someone on her side. "I am an innocent human being," she told the court. "I have committed no crime and I am treated like an outcast—a criminal. It is unjust, outrageous, uncivilized. It seems incredible that in a Christian community a defenseless woman can be treated in this manner."

Attorney O'Neill argued that the health department could not legally continue to hold Mary. "If the mere statement that a person is infected with germs is sufficient," he said, "then that person can be taken away from his or her home and family and locked up and imprisoned for life on North Brothers Island. That is what happened in this case."

His argument raised questions: How much power should a doctor have? How much power should a laboratory test have? Should the word of a medical doctor be sufficient to quarantine a person for life? Should the results of a laboratory test carry that much weight?

"Mary Mallon is in perfect physical condition," O'Neill told the judges. "She has never been obliged to receive the care and attention of a physician or surgeon."

In 1907, the year of Mary's arrest, 4,426 new cases of typhoid had been reported. Only two cases were traced back to a household where Mary happened to work. As far as O'Neill was concerned, the evidence against Mary was circumstantial. "This woman has been a victim of unfortunate circumstances in having been employed in houses where typhoid broke out," he said, "the disease having been unquestionably the result of conditions with which she had nothing to do."

By the time of Mary's court hearing in June 1909 the health department had identified five healthy carriers in New York City—and they knew for certain that more were loose in the city. Nationwide, fifty carriers had been identified. But Mary was the only one quarantined.

O'Neill jumped on this point. If other healthy carriers were loose in the city, if the law couldn't be applied equally and without bias—another protection under the Fourteenth Amendment—then why single out Mary Mallon?

Speaking for Riverside Hospital, Dr. Frederick Westmoreland explained that Mary was singled out for one reason. "Her occupation as a cook," he said. "The Department of Health concluded that the patient would be a dangerous person and a constant menace to the public health to be at large."

The health department did not broker a deal. Officials didn't offer Mary the opportunity to learn a new trade. They didn't offer her the opportunity to learn how not to infect others.

Instead, the officials argued that they had the right

to hold her because they had an obligation to protect the public's health. They submitted their laboratory tests as proof that she was a dangerous carrier.

O'Neill presented Mary's results from Ferguson Laboratories, which contradicted the health department's test results. The court would have to decide which reports to accept or whether to accept the laboratory reports at all. In a sense, the new science of bacteriology was also on trial.

The court proceeding lasted three hours. It's interesting to note that no witnesses testified against Mary, not even the members of the Walter Brown family, whose daughter had died. After the court adjourned, Mary returned to her bungalow on North Brother Island to await the judges' decision.

She may have known that her case was a long shot. She had already experienced the long, powerful arm of the New York City Department of Health.

Yet, the health department admitted that it was impractical and expensive to quarantine every carrier. "Where would we put them all?" Walter Bensel posed to a *New York Tribune* reporter. "Mallon is taking up valuable space in the Riverside Hospital and has caused us plenty of trouble and expense."

Her hopes may also have been bolstered by this

admission and by sympathetic stories and editorials that appeared in newspapers over the coming days. Not everyone believed that she should be quarantined. Some medical professionals called it unfair and suggested that she should be retrained in a new occupation.

A writer who called himself "New Thought Student" mocked the city's concern with Mary. "Why not send her other companions? Start a colony on some unpleasant island. Call it 'Uncle Sam's Suspects.' There collect Measles Sammy, Tonsillitis Joseph, Scarlet Fever Sally, Mumps Matilda, and Meningitis Matthew. Add Typhoid Mary, request the sterilized prayers of all religionized germ fanatics, and then leave the United States to enjoy the glorious freedom of the American flag under a medical monarchy."

Another interesting proposal came from a Michigan farmer. In a letter to Dr. Darlington, twenty-eight-year-old Reuben Gray wrote, "If Miss Mallon is not over ten years older and has nothing other than what you have found to bar her from the society of the world, and you will pardon her and get her into Michigan and see that the authorities of Michigan are not wise that she is here, and she will agree to become my wife, I will agree to become her husband."

But there was a caveat. "One thing she should be made aware of before the tie is bound and that is that I have been insane," said Gray. "But it was over three years ago, and I was pronounced cured then and never had a return of the disease."

Mary did not agree to become Reuben Gray's wife.

Three weeks later, on July 16, Mary had her answer. The court dismissed her writ of habeas corpus. Her detention on North Brother Island was not illegal, the court had decided. She would remain in the custody of the Board of Health of the City of New York.

The court explained the decision. "While the court deeply sympathizes with this unfortunate woman," said Justice Mitchell Erlanger, "it must protect the community against the recurrence of spreading the disease."

It was a terrible blow for Mary. Why were some healthy carriers allowed to roam free and she was not? She told a *New York World* reporter that there were "two kinds of justice in America" and that "she had not been given the benefit of the reasonable doubt which is allowed even to murderers."

"All the water in the oceans wouldn't clear me from this charge in the eyes of the Health Department," said Mary. "They want to make a showing. They want to get credit for protecting the rich, and I am the victim."

But she wasn't about to give up. "As there is a God in Heaven," she vowed to the reporter, "I will get justice, somehow, sometime."

For now, it seemed that the hard-working cook was destined to live out her life in quarantine on North Brother Island.

Chapter Thirteen

IN WHICH MARY LEARNS TO KEEP HER GERMS TO HERSELF

Mary remained on North Brother Island. From her bungalow, she wrote letters to Doctors Hermann Biggs and Josephine Baker and George Soper. The letters were, according to Biggs's biographer, "violently threatening."

In the letters, Mary vowed that if she were ever released from North Brother Island, she would take a gun and kill the doctors. We don't know how Soper and Biggs felt about the threat, but Baker later wrote, "I could not blame her for feeling that way."

"She could write an excellent letter, so far as composition and spelling were concerned," was all George Soper said. "She wrote in a clear, bold hand, and with remarkable uniformity."

On a snowy Monday, February 21, 1910, if Biggs, Baker, and Soper read the *New York Times,* they had cause to worry. There, buried on page 18, appeared a short article with the headline "TYPHOID MARY FREED."

✠

Two days earlier, the new health commissioner, Dr. Ernest J. Lederle, had offered Mary Mallon a deal: if she agreed not to cook, if she promised to take hygienic precautions to protect those with whom she came into contact, and if she reported monthly to the health department, she would be released.

Mary agreed, and Lederle handed her an affidavit to sign. He wanted her to put her promise in writing.

Mary did, writing, "I shall change said occupation upon being released from Riverside Hospital." She also agreed to report to the health department and "to take measures to protect any and all persons with whom I may come in contact from any infection."

To the last promise, she stubbornly added the phrase "which it is possible I may cause." No doctor would ever convince Mary that she was a typhoid carrier.

But Lederle was satisfied with her promise and signature—and possibly relieved to be rid of the woman.

"She had not been cured," he said. "But she has been taught how to take care of herself."

He told the *New York Times* reporter that Mary had learned the precautions she needed to take. "As long as she observes them [the precautions] I have little fear that she will be a danger to her neighbors," said Lederle.

He felt sympathy for Mary. "What will she do now?" asked Lederle. "She is a good cook and until her detention had always made a comfortable living. I really do not know what she can do." He added that he was trying to find work for her.

Who would hire Mary? Her name had been splattered in every major New York City newspaper and in newspapers across the country. How would she escape the stigma of "Typhoid Mary"?

In 1910 there were no government assistance programs such as unemployment benefits. Workers such as Mary were simply fired and replaced. No wages. No severance pay. She had no skills, other than cooking. No education. She had no family to take her in. All she had was Breihof.

But that wasn't Lederle's—or even the health department's—problem. They felt no obligation to help Mary. Once she signed the affidavit, their job was done. She was now the public's problem.

"She was incarcerated for the public's good," said Lederle, "and now it is up to the public to take care of her."

Some might say the health department no longer needed Mary. They had learned all they could from their experimental medications and laboratory tests. The doctors and health officials had become famous.

"She has been a great service to humanity," Dr. Josephine Baker would later write in her autobiography. "There have been many typhoid carriers recognized since her time, but she was the first charted case and for that distinction she paid in a life-long imprisonment."

Mary quietly packed up her few belongings. On February 19, 1910, she boarded the ferry that transported her across the East River to Manhattan.

The river was brown and icy. The current strong. The air cold and brisk. After nearly three years Mary Mallon was free.

✠

Over the next year, Mary reported regularly to the New York City Department of Health. She did not handle food for others. She did not work as a cook. She did not kill Biggs, Baker, or Soper.

But she found it difficult to support herself. As Lederle had promised, he found her work as a laundress, but washing clothes was physically demanding domestic work—and the lowest-paying. A laundress had to prepare her own starch, bleach, and detergents. She had to boil water and lift heavy pails.

Mary was now forty-one years old. For a person born in 1869, the average life expectancy was less than fifty years. (Life expectancy for the average forty-year-old today is about eighty.) In her previous job as a cook, Mary had been paid well, and she likely missed her usual wages. Good-paying jobs for women were scarce.

Those who knew her reported that she read a great deal and seldom missed the daily paper, usually the *New York Times.* Perhaps she saw her name in the December 2, 1910, *Times* article "GUIDE A WALKING TYPHOID FACTORY," about an upstate woodsman in the Adirondack Mountains who had infected thirty-six tourists with the disease. Two had died.

More than half of the article was devoted to Mary Mallon. The woodsman was not arrested. The New York State Department of Health said, "There is no state law by which a human carrier of typhoid bacilli can be kept from spreading contagion and disease."

The woodsman, known as "Typhoid John," agreed

to treatment, which the New York City Department of Health would provide as soon as it could find him a "boarding place." Unlike Mary Mallon, Typhoid John remained anonymous and soon disappeared from the headlines. Surely Mary must have wished she could disappear too.

The next spring, sometime in May 1911, Mary's friend Breihof suffered a heart attack. She helped him get to a hospital, where he later died. This was another huge blow to Mary. Although Breihof had betrayed her to Soper four years earlier, she had clearly forgiven him. Breihof had stood by her throughout her incarceration. He had delivered her specimens to the Ferguson Laboratories. And now he was dead.

Later that year, Mary turned to her attorney, George Francis O'Neill. She hired him to represent her in a lawsuit against New York City and the Board of Health for false imprisonment. She asked $50,000 in damages because she had been detained illegally, her civil rights violated.

The Board of Health, Mary contended, had made it impossible for her to follow her trade of cooking. Thus, the lawsuit said, "her chances of making a living are greatly reduced."

"The case," reported the *New York American,* "will demonstrate just how far the Board of Health powers go, and whether the department has the legal right to banish a person to confinement in absence of a court commitment."

"It is quite a problem," said O'Neill, "if a municipality can, without legal warrant, or due process of law, clap someone in jail upon the word of some medical man."

In filing the suit, O'Neill warned that the Board of Health's police power was dangerous. "If the Board of Health can act this way with anyone who is alleged to be a germ carrier, yet who never suffered from the disease," he said, "then it can put thousands upon thousands of persons who suffered at some time or another from typhoid fever in confinement because authorities agree for quite some time after recovery from typhoid, evidences of the disease remain in the system."

But the case never made it to court. O'Neill advised Mary that she had "no right for a civil action." In other words, the court dismissed her case because a judge decided it lacked merit.

✠

As Mary continued to honor the terms of her release, as she struggled to find work and to make ends meet, George Soper and others continued to lecture about

"Typhoid Mary." Time and again, Soper was credited with her discovery and detention. His name appeared in newspapers and professional journals.

On September 26, 1912, George Soper and Hermann Biggs addressed the International Hygiene Congress held in Washington, D.C. Throughout the conference, the words "Typhoid Mary" were evoked again and again. Mary's case was now known throughout the world, reported the *New York Times.*

For a private person such as Mary, who never talked about herself and who resented publicity, it was humiliating to open a newspaper and see her name. No doubt it felt like another peepshow.

Sometime that fall, after the conference—no one knows exactly when—Mary stopped reporting to the New York City Department of Health.

Despite the fact that the words "Typhoid Mary" appeared in New York City newspapers from time to time, no one noticed that Mary had slipped away. Not Soper. Not Biggs. Not Park. Not Baker.

Perhaps not even the readers of the *New York Times.* They may have missed the very last sentence in a November 29, 1914, article titled "Typhoid Carriers," on the second page of section C.

There it said, "It is reported that this woman, nicknamed 'Typhoid Mary,' has now been lost sight of. Will they find her again when she becomes the centre of another epidemic?"

No one knew where Mary Mallon was or what she was doing.

Chapter Fourteen

IN WHICH IT TAKES A SQUAD OF SANITARY POLICE

It was frightful. Typhoid fever was racing through Sloane Hospital for Women in Manhattan. The hospital had 8 physicians, 73 nurses, 75 employees, and 123 patients, all women, and a nursery of squalling newborn babies.

Twenty-five typhoid cases had broken out in January and February 1915. Twenty-four of the victims were doctors, nurses, or members of the hospital staff. One was a patient. Two people had died.

The hospital officials were stymied. How could such an epidemic happen? Sloane Hospital had an outstanding reputation. It was capably managed. It was clean. It attended to every sanitary measure and every rule of hygiene. It was a model hospital for the teaching of students in the College of Physicians and Surgeons.

And yet it had happened. It could have been far worse, but a vaccine against typhoid had been developed in 1911. A good number of the staff had been vaccinated or had natural immunity.

Still, the outbreak was an embarrassing dilemma for Edward Cragin, the hospital's chief physician, and the entire hospital staff—and a deadly one at that.

The Board of Health had checked the milk and other supplies but had failed to find the source of the infection.

The way George Soper tells the story, the hospital required the services of an expert epidemic fighter.

Cragin telephoned George Soper, asking him to come at once. It was "about a matter of great importance," Dr. Cragin told him.

Soper headed to the hospital right away. Cragin ushered him into his office. Behind closed doors, Cragin told him about the puzzling typhoid outbreak.

Soper questioned Cragin about the food and water supplies and the kitchen staff. Cragin admitted that the hospital had hired a new cook three months before the first outbreak, sometime around October 1914. She was a good cook. Efficient. Hard-working. She didn't talk much about herself, but everyone—doctors, nurses, staff members, and patients—enjoyed her cooking and her desserts. She was reliable. Never sick. She was well liked. Her name was Mrs. Brown.

The other employees had teased Mrs. Brown when the disease broke out. They had jokingly nicknamed her "Typhoid Mary."

Soper asked to meet Mrs. Brown, but she had left the building. Nobody knew where she had gone. But Cragin happened to have a letter from the cook. Might Soper recognize her handwriting?

Right away, possibly because of letters he had received from her over the years, Soper recognized the large, clear, bold handwriting, with its remarkably uniform letters.

"I saw at once that the cook was indeed Mary Mallon," he said.

✠

Dr. Josephine Baker told a different version of the story. In her version, she gave herself the credit for identifying Mary Mallon. As soon as Baker heard about the typhoid outbreak, she headed for the hospital and went straight to the kitchen.

"Sure enough, there was Mary earning her living

in the hospital kitchen and spreading typhoid germs among mothers and babies and doctors and nurses like a destroying angel," said Baker. She alerted authorities right away.

The *New York Sun* reported still another version. In order to find the cause of the outbreak, the hospital officials required its kitchen staff to supply stool samples in February, and Mary obliged.

Each of the laboratory specimens returned negative results, except for one. The cook's sample revealed "a faint trace" of the disease. "Before action could be taken, she mysteriously disappeared," reported the *Sun*.

But the stories of Baker, Soper, and the *Sun* all had the same ending: Mary slipped away from the hospital, unnoticed, before anyone could apprehend her.

✠

On Friday, March 26, 1915—nearly eight years to the day of her first arrest—a patrolman reported that a "veiled woman" had entered a house in Corona, a small town on Long Island.

The police officer recognized the woman's distinctive walk. It was "Typhoid Mary." Newspaper reporters would add dramatic details, saying that Mary was carrying a bowl of gelatin—"which she had lovingly prepared with her own lethal hands"—to her friend's house. They reported that the house was guarded by dogs.

Right away, the officer called for backup. A squad of sanitary police was dispatched to the Corona house, said the *New York Sun*. The police had been vaccinated against typhoid. They surrounded the house, and one officer rang the doorbell. On a side street, more police waited in an automobile, ready to whisk Mary away.

Nobody answered the door. Another officer found a ladder and propped it against the house. He climbed the ladder, slid open the window, let himself in, and faced a fearsome fox terrier and a bulldog.

Fortunately, the officer had brought along a piece of meat. He tossed it to the dogs. "The dogs offered a friendly truce," reported the *Sun*.

Some newspapers reported that the officer entered the bathroom just as Mary did. Other newspapers stated that the officer searched the upstairs room by room and found Mary cowering in the bathroom.

Mary, now forty-six years old, had no fight left.

"She was as strong as ever," said Soper, "but she had lost something of that remarkable energy and activity which had characterized her young days."

In 1915, after four years of freedom, Mary Mallon returned to her bungalow. "This time she had to go back under a life sentence to North Brother Island," said Baker. "It was Mary's tragedy that she could not trust us."

✣

Mary Mallon never said why she broke the conditions of her parole and took a job at the maternity hospital.

After Breihof died, we know that she struggled financially. Her former employment agencies wouldn't recommend her. No one would hire a cook named Mary Mallon.

But employers would hire Mary Brown and Marie Breshof and Mary Breihof and the other names that George Soper claimed Mary had used.

Under these names and possibly others, Soper said, Mary cooked in a Broadway restaurant, a hotel in Southampton, an inn at Huntington, a fashionable hotel in New Jersey, a sanatorium in New Jersey, and a cheap boarding house. He claimed that she infected others—including two children—but admitted that there was no record.

Is it possible that Mary simply didn't understand

that she shed the deadly bacteria, infecting others and making them sick?

Not according to George Soper. "Mary is not feeble, either in mind or body," he said. "She has been confronted with the facts [and] it is beyond belief that she has failed to grasp their significance."

Her temerity galled Soper. "She has had the assurance to go to a hospital, and of all places, a maternity hospital, to cook and possibly pollute the food of some 300 people."

✠

This time, few people felt sorry for Mary Mallon. "The chance was given to her five years ago to live in freedom," scolded the *New York Tribune* on March 29, 1915. "It is impossible to feel much commiseration for her." A few days later, the *New York Times* commented, "Here she was, dispensing germs daily with the food."

Within days, Mary's story made the front page of newspapers across the country. The *Tacoma Times* in Washington State claimed that the New York authorities had captured a modern witch who "uses far more scientific and more fateful magic."

"She requires no cauldron," wrote the *Tacoma Times*

on April 6, 1915. "She manufactures within herself the evil potions which she spread about her community."

George Soper had a suggestion for Mary. "I think that if she could get rid of the idea that she is being persecuted and would answer some questions concerning her history, that I might be able to help her in various ways."

He insisted that Mary had been treated fairly. Once again he used criminal terms to describe her situation. "She had been given her liberty and was out on parole," he said. "She had abused her privilege; she had broken her parole. She was a dangerous character and must be treated accordingly."

Soper was angry because Mary had endangered the lives of patients and the medical staff at Sloane Hospital. He was fed up because Mary had an obligation to help the medical and scientific community better understand germs and disease and contagion, and she had refused.

"She has never given me any help in the matter," he said. "She has never helped anyone in understanding her unfortunate condition, least of all herself."

As a result of her behavior, he added, "the world was not very kind to Mary."

Chapter Fifteen

IN WHICH A WEAKER SPIRIT MIGHT HAVE BEEN BROKEN

Once again, Mary made a life for herself on North Brother Island. Once again, she had a cottage of her own, food, a small dog, and freedom to walk the island.

Health officials described her as "a moody, caged jungle cat." But despite her refusal to cooperate, Dr. William Hallock Park told the *New Yorker* journalist Stanley Walker, they still tried to help her.

Park described how they tried to cure Mary by injecting her with five or six billion typhoid bacilli. "Into Mary went a billion germs hypodermically," reported Walker, "and they gave her pills containing the other billions."

Afterward, Park learned that Mary hadn't taken the

pills. She had hidden them and thrown them away. "The doctors admit that this treatment was to have been an experiment," said Walker. "It might not have worked."

The doctors also admitted that removing her gallbladder might not have cured her either. In some cases, surgery might have sent the germs into other organs, where they would have continued to breed.

"In any event, Mary didn't like the idea of having doctors tinker with her," concluded Walker. "A weaker spirit than Mary's might have been broken; a less intelligent hospital staff might have ruined her."

✠

Mary may have been unfriendly and angry toward health officials and those responsible for her removal to North Brother Island. She may not have given Soper the information he wanted. But there were others with whom Mary did talk and whom she befriended. These people remembered her as a woman who was friendly as long as you didn't pry into her past.

One man recalled that she made items out of beads, which she sold. "For a long time my mother had a choker of tiny blue beads that she had made," recalled George Edington, whose mother worked as a waitress in the doctors' dining room. He also recalled that Mary baked cakes that she sold to women who worked on the island.

It seems unlikely that the health department would have permitted Mary to bake cakes, but who knows? Perhaps Mary did bake cakes. Perhaps the women did buy them out of kindness or pity for the woman who had once made a good living as a cook. A cake is baked in a moderate oven—usually 350 degrees—and the temperature would have killed any typhoid germs.

To fill her hours, Mary read a great deal. She read such magazines as the *Saturday Evening Post, Harper's, Good Housekeeping,* and the *Ladies' Home Journal.* She enjoyed novels, especially the work of Charles Dickens. It was said she never missed reading the *New York Times.*

If she read the *Times* daily, Mary would have learned about other healthy carriers who had infected far more people than she had. In 1922, a farm worker named Tony Labella was forbidden to handle food. When Labella ignored the health department's orders, he caused an outbreak of eighty-seven typhoid cases, resulting in two deaths. He fled New York City and was found working in Newark, New Jersey, where he caused thirty-five more cases, resulting in three more deaths. After only two weeks of isolation, Labella was released. Six other known carriers also fled New York City that year.

In 1924, a bakery and restaurant owner named Alphonse Cotils was a known carrier. The health department forbade the baker to handle food, yet he was caught red-handed "preparing a strawberry shortcake."

A judge found him guilty but suspended his sentence. "I could not legally sentence this man to jail on account of his health," said the judge, "but I want to feel in suspending sentence that the burden is to be on the Department of Health to exercise its police powers if it so thinks necessary." The Department of Health never followed up on Cotils's probation terms.

In 1928 Mary may have met a Brooklyn confectioner sentenced to Riverside Hospital after he infected twenty-three people. Frederick Moersch had been identified as a carrier thirteen years earlier, after a typhoid outbreak that infected fifty-nine people was traced to his ice cream.

At that time, the health department treated Moersch leniently, determining that he warranted special treatment because he had four children and a wife in poor health. He received the same medical treatment as Mary during her first quarantine but was permitted to live at home. Like Mary, he was forbidden to handle food, and just as Mary had, he violated his probation and returned to the confectionery business in 1928.

Moersch left North Brother Island in 1944, but his years on the island garnered much less attention. No reporters tried to sneak photographs of him. No articles appeared in the newspapers. He wasn't called names such as "Typhoid Frederick."

Moersch worked as a hospital helper, paid by the city, at Riverside Hospital during his quarantine. After his release the city trained Moersch and continued to employ him at a Brooklyn hospital.

Like the other men who carried the disease, Moersch was treated differently from Mary by both the law and the newspapers.

Mary continued to write violently threatening letters to Hermann Biggs and Josephine Baker. To a reporter, Baker admitted that she felt uneasy after Mary had been released in 1910. "During the years she was at large, that little doubt would stay in the back of my mind," said Baker.

Though Mary lacked freedom, she made new friends and resumed friendships with others: Adelaide Offspring, the hospital nurse whom Mary had met in 1907; George Edington's mother, who worked in the doctors' dining room; Adele Leadley, who would become a loyal and longtime friend and with whom Mary corresponded; Tom Cane, a middle-aged man with an Irish accent who worked as a porter; the Lempe family, her longtime friends who lived on Long Island; and Father Michael Lucy, a Catholic priest.

✣

In 1918 Mary was offered work as a domestic at Riverside Hospital. She earned only about twenty dollars a month, but it was something. That year, the health authorities began to permit her to take day trips off the island.

On these occasions a laboratory worker noted that Mary dressed fashionably, wore a hat, and carried a purse. On her day off, she shopped and visited friends, most likely the Lempe family and later others. She always returned the same day, but she never told anyone where she went or with whom she visited.

Always a reliable worker, Mary worked her way up from "domestic" to "nurse" to "hospital helper" over the next seven years.

In 1925 a new resident physician, Dr. Alexandra Plavska, arrived on the island to intern at the hospital. Plavska hired Mary as a laboratory assistant and taught her the fundamentals of laboratory work.

Mary was never late. Each morning, she climbed the stairs to the laboratory, where she had her own desk and work area. For the most part, she prepared glass slides of specimens for the pathologists, kept records, and performed other necessary tasks such as bottle washing. For this, she earned about fifty dollars a month.

The work was important to Mary, and the two women became close friends. It wasn't the same as making a pudding or a cake, but laboratory work was interesting to Mary. "She was not brilliant, but she was thorough and careful," noted Stanley Walker in the *New Yorker.* "Her mind was eager and alert."

In 1927 Plavska completed her internship and left the island. Mary missed her friend, but often visited her and her young daughter, Julie, bringing small gifts and staying for dinner.

"She was a part of the family, and we really loved her," said Julie. "To me she was wonderful, so I see her with loving eyes, an older person but attractive, very warm and dear. She would always try to help in some way, you know, doing a hem of a dress or something like that." After Mary left, Julie and her mother scrubbed and boiled the dishes.

Mary would later describe Alexandra Plavska as a "beautiful person" who was always kind to her and who "believed in her." As Julie Plavska said, "It's a horrible thing because it wasn't her fault. She didn't put poison in the food. She just put a little of her bacteria."

✠

On September 23, 1932, Mary turned sixty-three. Two and a half months later, on December 4, Mary didn't show up for work. "She was always there practically before I opened the place, waiting for me," recalled Emma Goldberg Sherman, who worked as a bacteriologist in the hospital laboratory.

Concerned, Sherman left the laboratory and hurried to Mary's cottage. She knocked and knocked, and when Mary didn't answer, she opened the door. The cottage was dark, its curtains drawn. It also smelled bad and was in disarray.

"Miss Mallon! Miss Mallon!" Sherman called.

She heard a loud moan. Mary was lying on the floor, unable to move, paralyzed on her right side. She had suffered a stroke.

Mary was taken to the children's ward in Riverside Hospital, where she would remain bedridden and hospitalized for the next six years.

Alexandra and Julie Plavska continued to visit her. "Even though she had a stroke, she did recognize us," said Julie. "She just couldn't move and so on, and it was one of those things where she felt maybe she's not alone in the world. Which is a very bad thing, a very bad thing."

Father Michael Lucy and the Lempe family visited too, traveling by ferry across the East River to sit at Mary's bedside and keep her company.

On September 23, 1938, nearly six years after her stroke, Mary turned sixty-nine. Six weeks later she took a turn for the worse. She had pneumonia.

Adelaide Jane Offspring no longer lived and worked on the island, but she returned to care for her friend. Just after midnight on November 11, 1938, Mary died.

For the last time, Mary Mallon left North Brother Island. Her casket was ferried across the East River and taken to Saint Luke's Roman Catholic Church in the Bronx, where her funeral Mass was held.

Nine mourners attended the funeral. Reporters flocked to the church. They followed the mourners and the hearse to Saint Raymond's Cemetery, where Mary was laid to rest. Honoring her privacy, Mary's friends refused to identify themselves to the reporters present.

Alexandra Plavska and her daughter were among the mourners. "I remember the cemetery and the loneliness of it," recalled Julie years later. "We all need someone, and I think my mother answered her [Mary's] needs and that she was missing most of her life."

Mary's simple granite headstone is shown here at Saint Raymond's Cemetery, Bronx, New York. *Photograph by Joseph Bartoletti.*

Afterword

IN WHICH WE CONSIDER THE WRITING OF MARY'S LIFE

The summer after her stroke, on July 14, 1933, Mary sent for an attorney. She had saved more than $4,800 (about $63,100 today) from her hospital work. She wished to spell out how her estate would be divided and how her debts would be paid after she died. From her hospital bed, she made her final wishes known to her attorney.

From Mary's will, we can draw some conclusions. It suggests that she was a woman of faith: she left two hundred dollars to Father Michael Lucy, who had visited her. It suggests she cared about the less fortunate: she gave two hundred and fifty dollars to Catholic Charities of the Archdiocese of New York.

Her will shows that she had friends about whom

she cared deeply: she left two hundred dollars to Willie Lempe and her clothing and personal effects to Willie's mother, Mary; she left two hundred dollars to Alexandra Plavska.

Mary bequeathed the remainder of her estate—$4,172.05 after her debts were paid—to her good friend Adelaide Jane Offspring. Mary paid for her funeral, her burial, and her headstone herself.

Mary's death was reported widely in newspapers, medical periodicals, and bulletins of public health departments. It angered George Soper that so many of these reports contained misinformation. He blamed the misfortune on a "flippant" article written by a "free-lance journalist" and published in an "allegedly smart periodical." The article is "Profiles: Typhoid Carrier No. 36," written by Stanley Walker, published in the January 26, 1935, *New Yorker.*

Soper scolded the other writers for relying on Walker's article. He chastened them for not taking the time to look up his professional papers in the *Journal of the American Medical Association* and the *Military Surgeon,* in which he described his investigation.

These writers, Soper said, "rob me of whatever credit belongs to the discovery of the first typhoid carrier to be found in America and (to the time of her death) the most famous carrier anywhere."

Although George Soper found Walker's article "the source of much of the misinformation," a close read of the article does not reveal any more misinformation or mistakes than other writers' articles do, including Soper's own work. Among Soper's mistakes is the misidentification of the Oyster Bay family, an error that still appears today in many articles and books.

Soper's main objection may have been that the five-page *New Yorker* article devotes a scant two paragraphs to him and his investigative work and that the article didn't give him sole credit as Mary's "discoverer."

"Suffice it to say that I did not stumble upon her in the course of routine duties as an employee of the Health Department or as a blind disciple of Robert Koch," wrote Soper. Adding insult to injury may have been that Josephine Baker was given equal billing and complete credit for Mary's second arrest.

Perhaps to set the record straight or to have the final word, Soper wrote "The Curious Career of Typhoid Mary." Soper proved to be a masterful storyteller. Adding new details that flesh out Mary's life, he crafted a moralistic and cautionary tale. The paper was published in the *Bulletin of the New York Academy of Medicine* in October.

Was George Soper a bad guy? Despite his vainglorious tendencies, he seems to have had a genuine interest in improving the lives of others and making the world a safer and more sanitary place. He devised comprehensive plans for the ventilation system for New York City's subway system and for the city's sewage disposal. He developed plans for Chicago's water supply and sewage disposal.

After the sinking of the *Titanic,* he completed a study of drifting ice in the Atlantic. He traveled abroad to study health and sanitation methods in European cities and returned home with ideas for fundamental changes in New York's street cleaning, refuse collection, and waste disposal. Later, he was named managing director of the American Society for the Control of Cancer, now known as the American Cancer Society. He served actively until 1928 and thereafter as a consultant.

When he died, in 1948, Soper left behind his wife, Eloise, and two sons, George and Harvey. His obituary noted his many accomplishments, but it also highlighted his "discovery" of Typhoid Mary and gave him credit for her arrest. "Because of her confinement, thanks to Dr. Soper, millions of people lived in greater security," said his *New York Times* obituary.

✠

Like Soper, Dr. S. Josephine Baker also had a genuine interest in improving the lives of others. She served as the first director of New York's Bureau of Child Hygiene. In that position, Baker created policies that helped reduce the instances of infant death. Across the country, thirty-five states implemented her school health program.

The "S" stood for Sara, but Baker preferred her middle name, Josephine. She was a feminist, a suffragist, a lecturer, and the author of fifty journal articles, two hundred articles for popular magazines, and five books: *Healthy Babies* (1920), *Healthy Mothers* (1920), *Healthy Children* (1920), *The Growing Child* (1923), and *Child Hygiene* (1925).

Dr. Baker seems to have been less obsessed with Mary Mallon. In her three-hundred-page autobiography, *Fighting for Life,* Baker devoted only six pages to Mary. She reflected on their brief acquaintance, saying, "I learned to like her and to respect her point of view."

Baker retired in 1923 and moved to New Jersey, where she lived with her life partner, novelist Ida Wylie. Baker died in 1945. Her lengthy *New York Times* obituary noted her many accomplishments but did not mention Typhoid Mary.

✠

Today, if North Brother Island has any secrets to tell about Mary Mallon, it guards them closely. The island is overgrown with kudzu, porcelain berry, poison ivy, weeds, and thickets. Riverside Hospital and other buildings are crumbling or lie in ruins. The tiny cottage where Mary lived for nearly twenty-six years is gone.

The island is now a sanctuary for nesting herons. It's nearly impossible to visit. (I tried.) If the New York City Department of Parks and Recreation grants you permission, you have to charter a boat between the months of November and February, when the herons aren't nesting.

Mary Mallon isn't revealing any secrets either. Other than the six-page unpublished letter she wrote to the editor of the *New York American* in 1909, she didn't talk or write about her life publicly, to the best of our knowledge. If she talked about her life to her friends, they didn't betray her confidences. Mary remained a woman of great strength, fiercely private and independent throughout her life and her final years.

We are left to learn about her from what others say about her; from the way contemporaneous newspapers such as the *New York American* portrayed her and reported what she said and did; from how people such as George Soper and Josephine Baker related their encounters with her; and from what outstanding scholars such Judith Walzer Leavitt and Priscilla Wald have determined about her and her world.

There's a danger in writing a person's life from a historical vantage point, for hindsight can be smug. For example, as I was shaping this story, guided by the facts, I could see Mary Mallon approaching her fate. If only she'd understood what George Soper and the others were telling her. If only she'd understood the facts of germ theory. If only she'd trusted science. If only the health department had offered her retraining or different work. If only she hadn't accepted that job at Sloane Hospital. If only the health department had treated her the same as they treated other carriers. If only . . .

✠

I couldn't visit North Brother Island, but I did walk the neighborhoods where Mary lived and worked in New York City. I started at 688 Park Avenue, where she worked for the Bowne family, and walked down to

Third Avenue, just below Thirty-third Street. I stood across the street, where Soper might have skulked as he watched and waited for Mary.

Another weekend, I headed to Oyster Bay, Long Island, to see where the Thompson house once stood. The house has been torn down. It's now the site of a school administration building and a parking lot. New houses obscure the bay, but seagulls wheel overhead and complain, and the smell of the ocean is strong.

From Oyster Bay, I drove back across the Throgs Neck Bridge. I found Saint Raymond's Cemetery in the Bronx. I stopped at the office for a map of the old cemetery, and wound my way to Mary's grave. It's marked by a simple granite headstone that bears the words MARY MALLON, DIED NOV. 11, 1938 and, at the bottom, JESUS MERCY.

I sat cross-legged on the grass and thought about Mary. Mary Mallon was a complex, complicated human being. She wasn't an unthinking, unfeeling half-human machine or a witch, as the health department and the media portrayed her. One day she was a hard-working and well-respected cook; the next day she was not. She believed she was a kidnapped woman, insulted and robbed of her freedom, her reputation, her livelihood, and her identity. No wonder Mary's will includes the words "considering the uncertainty of this life."

I thought about all I had learned. This I know for sure: Life is, as Mary says, uncertain. As a society and as individuals, we must protect healthy people from disease. We must also treat those suffering from disease in an intelligent, humane, and compassionate way. We need to be rational and keep our fears in check.

PHOTO ALBUM

Mary Mallon, as portrayed during her court hearing. *New York American,* June 30, 1909. *Courtesy Library of Congress.*

In this photograph, taken between 1900 and 1910, laundry stretches on a clothesline above a tenement yard. By 1900 there were 82,652 tenement buildings on the Lower East Side of Manhattan. *Courtesy Library of Congress.*

Morning Roll Call of Street Sweepers at the Section Station.

New York City street cleaners line up for the morning roll call in 1923. *Courtesy New York City Municipal Archives Collection.*

Dr. George A. Soper graduated from Columbia University's School of Mines in 1899. *Courtesy University Archives, Columbia University in the City of New York.*

STARTING OUT FOR A DAY'S WORK, *CIRCA* 1912

Dr. Josephine Baker, pictured here in 1912, drives a motorcar on her rounds in New York City. *Published in Baker's autobiography,* Fighting for Life.

Dr. Josephine Baker, known as Dr. Joe to her friends, is pictured here in 1925, at age fifty-two. *Courtesy Library of Congress.*

BELOW: A newspaper artist depicted Mary tending a pot of steaming skulls. New York American, *June 30, 1909. Courtesy New York Public Library.*

A newspaper sketch artist depicted Mary's arrest on March 20, 1907, when it took four policemen to strong-arm her into the ambulance waiting to whisk her away to Willard Parker Hospital. New York American, *June 30, 1909. Courtesy New York Public Library.*

North Brother Island can be seen in the distance in this photograph, taken from the Bronx shoreline between 1931 and 1937. The East River currents made it treacherous to swim or navigate small boats there. Once the home of Riverside Hospital, the abandoned island is now a sanctuary for nesting birds. *Courtesy New York Public Library.*

Mary's cottage on North Brother Island. *Courtesy New York City Municipal Archives.*

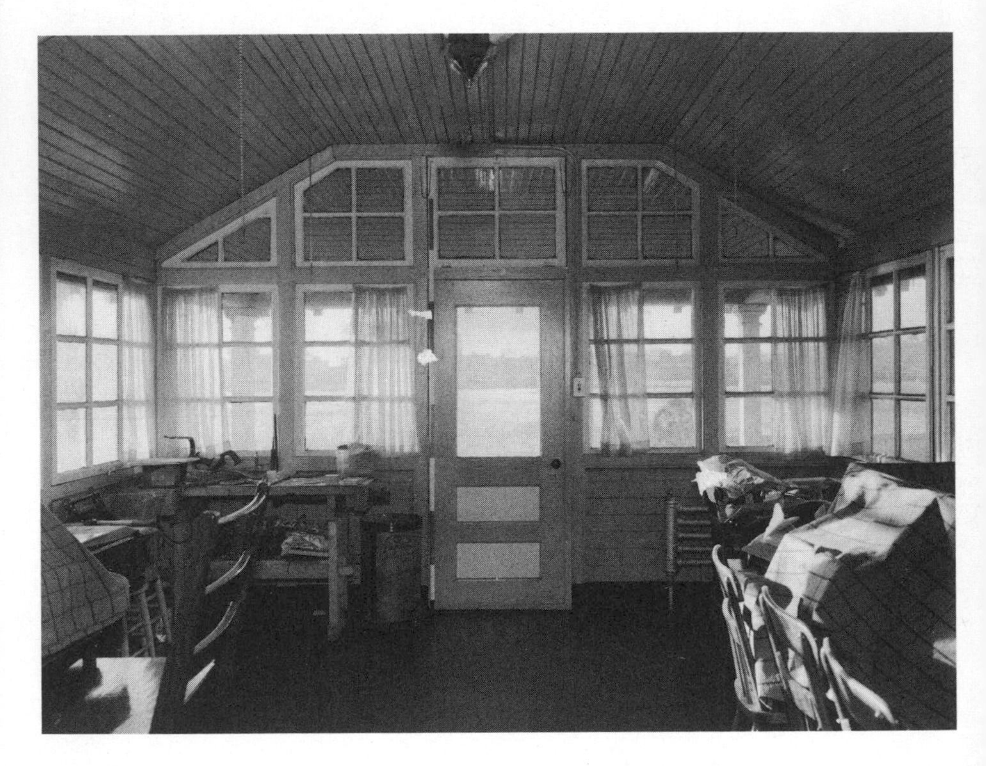

The cottage interior shows tables, chairs, a sewing machine covered with a towel, and skeins of wool. It was said that Mary kept the shades and curtains drawn so that snooping photographers wouldn't be able to sneak a picture. *Courtesy New York City Municipal Archives.*

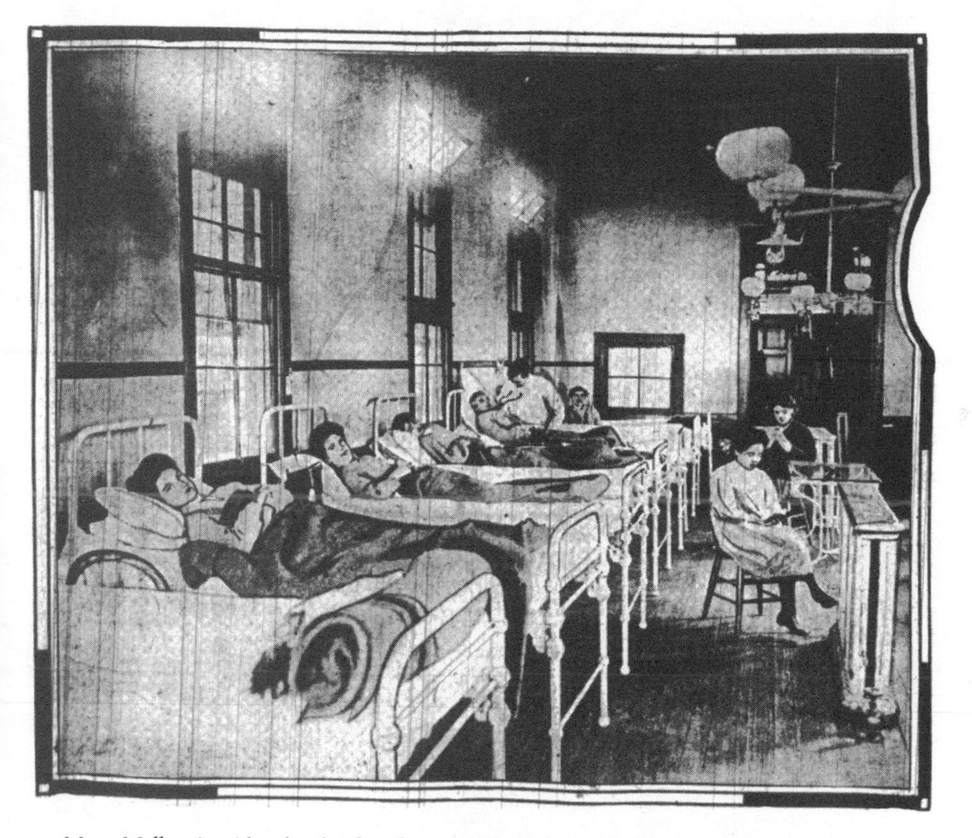

Mary Mallon is said to be the first figure on the left, lying in a cot in the convalescent ward, possibly at Riverside Hospital on North Brother Island. In her letter to the editor of the *New York American,* Mary denied Dr. William Hallock Park's claim that she was "segregated with the typhoid patients." "There is nobody on this *island* that has typhoid," said Mary. The photo appears to have been enhanced with illustration. New York American, *June 30, 1909. Courtesy New York Public Library.*

Mary Mallon, possibly the fourth woman from the right, is shown with other patients on North Brother Island. New York American, *June 30, 1909. Courtesy New York Public Library.*

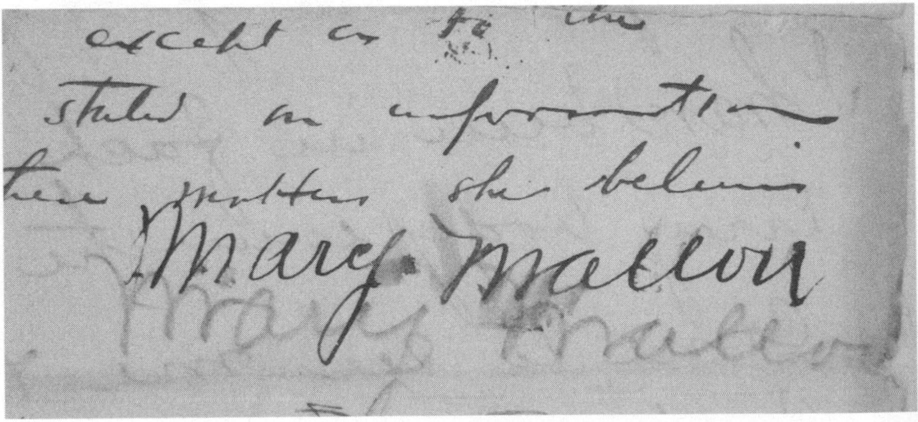

Mary Mallon's signature appears in large, clear handwriting at the bottom of her undated letter to the editor of the *New York American*. The letter is held at the New York County Courthouse, New York City. *Photograph by the author.*

2
with grief & trouble my eyes began to
twitch & the left eye lid became paralyzed
would not move remained in that condi-
-tion for six months there was an eye
Specialist visited the Island 3 & 4
times a week he was never asked to
visit me I did not even get a cross
for my eye had to hold my hand
on it whilst going about & at night
tie a bandage on it In December
when Dr Wilson took charge he came
to me & I told him about it he said
that was news to him & that he would
send me his Electrick battery but he
never sent; However my eye got better
thanks to the Almighty God ~~& no thanks~~
In spite of the medical staff Dr Wilson
ordered me Urotropin I got that on & off for
a year sometimes the had it & sometimes

George Soper wrote that her "clear, bold hand" had "remarkable uniformity" and that her composition and excellent spelling showed intelligence. *Photograph by the author.*

This 1909 advertisement capitalizes on the public's fear of the contagious nature of typhoid fever. Typhoid germs do not float in the air, waiting to land on victims. Lime juice will not kill the germs. *Courtesy U.S. National Library of Medicine.*

This 1920 illustration shows that the public at that time still didn't understand germ theory—and that it feared domestic servants. Here, a shrouded Death stands with a scythe, rubbing his hands, together in anticipation, as a maid sweeps germs into the air. *Courtesy U.S. National Library of Medicine.*

TIMELINE OF EVENTS IN MARY'S LIFE

1845–1850.

Great Irish Famine: A potato blight destroys two-thirds of Ireland's staple food. An estimated one million people die from starvation and starvation-related diseases. Two million emigrate.

September 23, 1869.

Mary Mallon is born in Cookstown, County Tyrone, Ireland. Her parents are John Mallon and Catherine Igo. It was customary for Irish women to keep their maiden names after marriage.

1883.

Mary immigrates alone to New York City some time before or after her fifteenth birthday. She lives with her aunt and uncle until their deaths.

1897–1900.

For three years, Mary works for a Mamaroneck, New York, family that has a summer home on Long Island. A case of typhoid fever develops in a young man about ten days after his arrival at the house.

Winter 1901–2.

Mary cooks for a New York City family for eleven months. One month after her arrival, the family's laundress develops typhoid fever.

Summer 1902.

Mary works for the family of New York lawyer J. Coleman Drayton. The Draytons take her to their vacation home. While there, four members of the Drayton family and five servants develop typhoid fever.

Summer 1904.

Mary works for the Henry Gilsey household in Sands Point, New York, for nine months. Four newly employed servants develop typhoid fever.

August 1906.

Mary cooks for the Charles Elliot Warren family in Oyster Bay, New York. Three family members and three servants develop typhoid fever shortly after Mary is hired.

Autumn 1906.

Two weeks after Mary is hired as a cook for the George Kessler family, in Tuxedo Park, New York, the laundress becomes ill.

Winter 1907.

Mary cooks for the Walter Bowen family of 688 Park Avenue, New York City. Two months later a laundress falls sick with typhoid fever, followed by the Bowens' twenty-one-year-old daughter. The daughter dies in February.

March 1907.

George Soper tracks Mary to the Bowens' Park Avenue townhouse and later to August Breihof's rooming house on Third Avenue. Soper attempts to interview Mary.

March 20, 1907.

Dr. Sara Josephine Baker arrests Mary at 688 Park Avenue. Mary is held in isolation at Willard Parker Hospital. Sometime thereafter, she is removed to Riverside Hospital on North Brother Island.

April 2, 1907.

Mary's story is leaked to the *New York American*.

April 1907.

Soper delivers a paper, "The Work of a Chronic Typhoid Germ Distributor," before the Biological Society of Washington, D.C.

June 1908.

William Hallock Park presents a paper, "Typhoid Bacilli Carriers," before a session of the American Medical Association. At this session, the term "typhoid Mary" is first used.

July 1908 to April 1909.

Mary arranges for Ferguson Laboratories to analyze her samples.

June 20, 1909.

The *New York American* publishes a double-page spread and identifies Mary Mallon. On or around this date, attorney George Francis O'Neill offers to represent Mary.

June 28, 1909.

O'Neill submits a writ of habeas corpus to the court.

July 16, 1909.

Mary is remanded to North Brother Island.

February 19, 1910.

Mary is released from Riverside Hospital after she signs an affidavit promising not to cook for others and to report monthly to the health department.

December 1911.

Mary sues New York City for damages; the suit is dropped.

October 1914.

Mary (as Mary Brown) is hired as a cook at Sloane Hospital for Women.

January 1915.

Typhoid fever breaks out at Sloane Hospital.

March 26, 1915.

The health department apprehends Mary for the second time; she is sent back to North Brother Island.

March 1, 1918.

Mary is employed by the city as a domestic at Riverside Hospital.

June 11, 1918.

Mary is granted off-island day privileges.

July 1919.

Soper publishes the article "Typhoid Mary."

1923.

Mary begins works as a laboratory assistant.

1925 to 1927.

Dr. Alexandra Plavska befriends Mary. They work together for two years.

December 4, 1932.

Mary suffers a stroke and is bedridden.

November 11, 1938.

Mary dies.

November 12, 1938.

Mary's funeral is held at Saint Luke's Roman Catholic Church in the Bronx; she is buried in Saint Raymond's Cemetery, also in the Bronx.

October 1939.

Soper publishes "The Curious Career of Typhoid Mary."

SOURCES

This is a work of nonfiction.

In order to tell Mary's story as accurately as possible, I relied on the sources cited in this section and cross-listed in the bibliography. I have tried to keep my citations as concise as possible. I cite all quoted material and specific information, including those places where I state what a person is thinking or feeling, based on verifiable fact or reason. Where necessary for clarity, I have adjusted the tense. I have omitted citations for facts that are widely known and accepted. My abbreviated citations include the author, the source if more than one author, and the page number. Complete information can be found in the bibliography.

Where applicable, I offer my reasoning and supporting sources, including those who have drawn the same conclusions and in whose steps I have followed. Despite my research and the time spent with Mary, she is still the authority on her own life. In her own way, Mary wrote her own life.

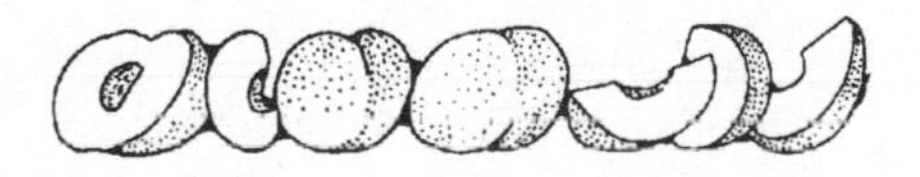

Chapter 1

page 3 *She could not manage without one* and *2.3 million:* Sutherland, 45. Sutherland tells us that "one woman who managed without a cook for just one week found herself 'broken down, sick & in bed.'"

A telephone conversation with Dorothy Simons, maternal aunt of Mrs. Warren's grandson, Shannon Lord Meany III, provided background information on the Warrens, as did the transcript to the BBC *Timewatch* docudrama "Typhoid Mary."

4 *A good servant wasn't uppity:* Sutherland 45; Husband and O'Loughlin, 118. See bibliography for more sources consulted on the general qualities of a good servant.

If a servant was smarter: Husband and O'Loughlin, 35.

employers were more equal: Sutherland, 123.

A good servant didn't complain: Husband and O'Loughlin, 118.

a specific race, nationality, and religion: Sutherland, 26.

5 *"Send me a cook":* Lovering, "Typhoid Mary," BBC *Timewatch,* transcript, 7.

Mary had worked for some: The high-society families Mary worked for included that of the New York lawyer J. Coleman Drayton.

forty-five dollars: Soper, "Curious Career," 701.

$1,180 today: "Measuring Worth."

double the salary for the same worker: Sutherland, 108. In "Typhoid Mary," p.12, Soper notes that "the more we pay the less we know about our servants."

6 *she'd simply send her back:* Lovering, "Typhoid Mary," BBC *Timewatch,* transcript, 7.

she was thirty-seven years old: Details about Mary are found in Soper's "Work of a Chronic Typhoid Germ Distributor," "Typhoid Mary," and "Curious Career."

More than 80 percent: Blessing, 551.

6 *touted them as excellent workers:* Lynch-Brennan, 81–82.

"quick wit" . . . "as a rule, honest": Ibid.

CHAPTER 2

8 *large yellow house with tall windows:* Photographs. Oyster Bay Historical Society and personal research trip to Oyster Bay, October 7, 2013. The house is no longer there. It has been torn down and replaced with administrative buildings and a high school parking lot.

9 *As Mary settled into:* Sutherland, 93–94.

"intelligent" and *"violent temper":* Soper, "Typhoid Mary," 4.

"noncommunicative" and *"with a glare":* Soper, "Curious Career," 711.

10 *no hot-water faucet:* Conclusion drawn from the facts of the case and from Soper's "Chronic Typhoid Germ Distributor" (p. 2020), in which he mentions that the kitchen had one faucet. At this time, other sources state that the stove was used to heat water.

all-purpose store-bought bar soap: Hill, 61–62.

11 *clean the hall: Cassell's Household Guide,* 170.

"kitchen piano": "Early 20th Century American Kitchens." This interesting website shows an advertisement for a kitchen piano.

ice cost about five cents: New York Times, "Women Discuss Ice Question," 2.

12 *nothing was wasted:* Sutherland, 93.

Thrift was an art: Gregory, 42–44.

13 *"The largest and finest peaches": Long-Islander,* August 31, 1906, 4.

14 *To her employers:* Mary's refusal to talk about her past has been noted by those who knew her: George Soper, other health authorities mentioned in these pages, and Emma Rose Goldberg Sherman.

we know that she was born: Mary's death certificate; see Mallon. See also Leavitt, *Typhoid Mary: Captive,* 163.

14 *she boarded a steamship:* Leavitt, *Typhoid Mary, Captive,* 163.

15 *10 percent of its population:* Ryan, 525. Another 10 percent emigrated.

73 percent of her peers: Perlman, 53–54.

10 percent below: Given that Mary immigrated to America at about age fifteen in 1883, she probably learned to read and write in Ireland. Therefore, the 1880 census reflects her school age group. In "Curious Career" (p. 698), for example, Soper calls Mary intelligent and remarks on her excellent spelling and composition.

"Often the children": New York World, "I'm Persecuted! Is Plaintive Plea of Typhoid Mary," 18.

16 *Was she escaping:* The pain and power of these possibilities are from Melissa V. Harris-Perry's *Sister Citizen,* 101–33, which has helped inform this book.

"*All that is necessary": Long-Islander,* August 24, 1906, 6.

17 *spiking as high as 105 degrees:* Details about typhoid fever symptoms drawn from Mayo Clinic and other U.S. government medical sites.

18 *Within the week:* Soper, "Chronic Typhoid Germ Distributor," 2019. In this 1907 paper, Soper notes, "At the time of the outbreak, no other case was known. None followed." However, the *Long-Islander* newspaper (August 31, 1906) reports that Miss Carrie Bryant, daughter of Frederick Bryant, Oyster Bay, died from typhoid fever and that her funeral was held on August 24, 1906. Thirteen years later Soper ("Typhoid Mary," 3) writes that ten known cases existed.

Warrens packed up: New York Times, "Five Ill in One Household." In "Chronic Typhoid Germ Distributor" (1907), Soper doesn't name the banker. In "Typhoid Mary" (1919), he identifies the banker as "General William Henry Warren," and in "The Curious Career of Typhoid Mary" (1939) as Charles Henry Warren. The correct name is Charles Elliot Warren. This was determined after consulting the 1906 New York City directory; *Who's Who;* a letter written by Charles Elliot Warren and published in an advertisement in *The Motor Way,* July 5, 1906: 28, and a telephone conversation with Dorothy Simons, upstate New York (the maternal aunt of Charles E. Warren's grandson, Shannon Lord Meany III) on October 4, 2013. The *New York Times* also misstates that members of the Charles Elliot

Warren family were stricken in Dorchester Bay, Massachusetts, not the near-rhyme Oyster Bay, Long Island. However, after consulting and comparing the aforementioned sources, I feel confident that the stricken family was that of Charles Elliot Warren. The BBC *Timewatch* documentary "Typhoid Mary" also identifies the family as that of Charles Elliot Warren.

CHAPTER 3

20 *the grass grew high:* The gardener was one of the servants stricken. It takes a month to recover from typhoid fever.

Mr. and Mrs. George Thompson: Soper, "Typhoid Mary," 2. Soper first identified the house owners twelve years after the outbreak.

vacationed at their cottage: Wenzell, "Typhoid Mary," BBC *Timewatch,* transcript, 4; Hammond, 9. Hammond states that the Thompsons learned about the typhoid outbreak when they returned home in time to enjoy the Vanderbilt Cup Races in October 1906.

news about the Warren family: New York Times, "Five Ill in One Household," 1.

21 *the stigma of typhoid:* Soper, "Chronic Typhoid Germ Distributor," 2019, and "Typhoid Mary," 3.

condemned or even burned down: Long-Islander, "The Water Supply Question." 1; Soper, "Curious Career," 700. Here, Soper credits himself with the burning of one such property in the Adirondacks.

officials were just as concerned: Soper, "Chronic Typhoid Germ Distributor," 2019.

22 *health department officials got busy:* Ibid., 2019–20. In this source, Soper provides the details on how an outbreak might occur and the steps the investigators took.

24 *the epidemic would have been much greater:* Ibid., 2020.

No harmful bacteria were found: Ibid., 2019.

"Miss Margaret Warren": New York Times, "Five Ill in One Household,"1.

24 *health department officials determined:* Soper, "Chronic Typhoid Germ Distributor," 2020. Again, the funeral of Carrie Bryant is not mentioned.

Not for Mrs. Thompson: Wenzell, "Typhoid Mary," BBC *Timewatch* transcript, 5.

Chapter 4

25 *townspeople continued to speculate:* Soper, "Chronic Typhoid Germ Distributor," 2020. Here Soper mentions Mr. Thompson's concern. In the BBC *Timewatch* docudrama "Typhoid Mary," the Thompsons' grandson Tom Wenzell notes that it was Mrs. Thompson who wasn't satisfied with the investigation.

26 *for she hired Soper:* Soper, "Curious Career," 699. Here Soper states that the house belonged to Mrs. George Thompson and that she hired him. Eighteen years earlier, he states that Mr. Thompson hired him. In the BBC *Timewatch* transcript "Typhoid Mary," the Thompsons' grandson Tom Wenzell confirms that the house belonged to his grandmother and that she hired Soper (p. 6).

United States Army Sanitary Corps: Wald, 68.

27 *160 pounds of food:* Melosi, 19–20; Gore, 332; Davies, 32.

28 *67 percent: Annual Report of the Board of Health of the Department of Health of the City of New York for the Year Ending December 31, 1906,* 335. Although the incidences of the disease were fewer, the fatality rate was about the same, 18 percent.

3,467 cases: Soper, "Curious Career," 699. Confirmed in *Annual Report,* 473.

He arrived at the Thompson house: Soper, "Chronic Typhoid Germ Distributor," 2021. In all three accounts Soper states that he began his investigation in the winter of 1906 or 1906–7. However, as Leavitt notes in *Typhoid Mary: Captive to the Public's Health* (p. 238, fn. 3), Soper isn't clear about when he arrived in Oyster Bay. In one account he says he arrived four months after the August outbreak and in another more than six months after the outbreak.

29 *"I was disappointed":* Soper, "Curious Career," 700.

30 *"They were sometimes taken":* Soper, "Chronic Typhoid Germ Distributor," 2020.

31 *Each case:* Ibid.

32 *"Here was by all means":* Ibid., 2021. Soper gives similar accounts in "Curious Career," 701, and "Typhoid Mary," 4.

33 *freezing didn't kill:* Soper, "Curious Career," 702.

the intestinal tract: "Epidemiology," 12; Mann.

"I suppose no better way": Soper, "Curious Career," 702.

"No doubt her hands": Ibid., 704.

After using the toilet: Ibid.

34 *soap and 140-degree water:* "S. typhi."

Water that hot can cause: Burn Foundation.

"If this woman could be found": Soper, "Chronic Typhoid Germ Distributor," 2021.

But Soper had her name: Soper, "Curious Career," 701.

Chapter 5

36 *owned by a man:* Soper, "Typhoid Mary," 4. Here, and in "Chronic Typhoid Germ Distributor" and "Curious Career," Soper details his detective work.

37 *Dr. Robert Koch:* "Robert Koch, 1843–1910."

"healthy carriers": Leavitt, "Typhoid Mary Strikes Back," 558; "Robert Koch, 1843–1910."

38 *George Soper was certain:* Ibid., 701. Here, Soper also says, "Nothing of the kind had been done in America."

His name would go down: Soper did go on to write papers, be interviewed in newspapers, and lecture at important medical conferences. His desire for fame is drawn from his accomplishments, his writings, and the scolding he gave to the author (believed to be Stanley Walker of the *New Yorker*) of a "flippant article" that, Soper said, robbed him of "whatever credit belongs to the discovery of the first typhoid carrier to be found in America." See Soper, "Discovery of Typhoid Mary," 37.

38 *"Few housekeepers seem to know":* Soper, "Typhoid Mary," 4. Here, "housekeepers" means female employers. As noted in the transcript of "Typhoid Mary," BBC *Timewatch,* 3–4. Lovering confirms that her grandmother was one such housekeeper.

39 *"Sometimes it appear [ed]":* Soper, "Typhoid Mary," 5.

"a family that consisted": Soper, "Chronic Typhoid Germ Distributor," 2022.

"In every instance": Ibid.

40 *Each time, the source:* Soper, "Curious Career," 702.

"Mr. Drayton told me": Ibid., 703.

Drayton was naturally immune: Ibid.

41 *"She had never been suspected":* Ibid.

Mr. Walter Bowne: New York Times, "Died" 7. Soper misspelled the Bowne name as "Bowen" in his writings, a mistake that has been repeated in many articles and books.

"The only child": Soper, "Curious Career," 704. As many as 4,500 cases of typhoid fever were reported each year in New York City. See "Epidemiology."

"I felt a good deal": Ibid.

"I was as diplomatic": Ibid.

42 *"I had made a bad start":* Ibid.

She told him: Soper, "Typhoid Mary," 7, and "Curious Career," 705.

"I told her": Soper, "Curious Career," 704.

43 *he wanted specimens:* Ibid.

"Apparently, Mary did not": Soper, "Curious Career," 704. This source describes the near run-in with the carving fork; "Chronic Typhoid Germ Distributor" does not.

Chapter 6

44 *"I felt rather lucky":* Soper, "Curious Career," 704.

44 *"She was five feet six":* Ibid., 698. In 1907, the average height for a woman was five feet four inches, and the average height for a man was five feet nine inches. See Hathaway and Foard, *Heights and Weights of Adults in the United States,* Home Economics Research Report No. 10 (Washington, D.C.: U.S. Department of Agriculture, 1960), 4.

45 *"at the height of her physical":* Soper, "Curious Career," 698.

"pious, pure, domestic": Welter, 152. These views of "true womanhood" were still dominant in 1907 but were challenged by the emergence of the "New Woman." The New Woman was educated and pursued legal and political rights as well as work outside the home. But she still hailed from the middle and upper classes. See White, 18–25.

"Nothing was so distinctive": Soper, "Curious Career," 698.

46 *society had strict ideas about womanhood:* Wald, 86, 97.

more than 50 percent of women: "Movements for Political & Social Reform, 1870–1914." Ireland's Great Famine (1845–1850) resulted in social and economic changes in Mary's homeland. Young women delayed marriage or didn't marry at all. Mary's marital status was similar to her peer group in Ireland. In 1901 more than half of all women ages 25 to 34 remained unmarried. Young girls and unmarried women were encouraged to emigrate.

47 *"I expected to find a person":* Soper, "Typhoid Mary," 6.

"I supposed that she would be glad": Ibid.

48 *He felt certain that he had gathered:* Soper, "Chronic Typhoid Germ Distributor," 2022. Soper describes his certainty as "believing."

"a menace to the public health": Ibid.

"As a matter of fact": Soper, "Curious Career," 704.

49 *"I found that Mary":* Ibid.

50 *"She was spending the evenings":* Ibid., 704–5. Leavitt and others state that Mary was living with Briehof.

50 *"I should not care to see":* Soper, "Curious Career," 705.

51 *From census records, it seems:* According to the 1907 New York City directory, the only Breihof with a name that begins with the letter *A* at this rooming house address is August Breihof, whose occupation is given as a police officer. According to the U.S. Census Reports, tenth census, June 1, 1880, August Breihof was born in 1856 in Manhattan and was married and living in Philadelphia, where he worked as a tailor. A wife and three children are listed on the census. After that, Breihof's trail disappears until he shows up twenty-three years later in the 1903 New York City directory.

Some claim that Mary lived: See, for example, Leavitt, *Typhoid Mary: Captive,* 108–9.

From Soper's accounts, we know: The first time Soper recounts the story of finding Mary in 1907, he doesn't mention Breihof. In 1919 Soper simply calls the man "Mary's friend." Twenty years later, Soper's story is noticeably more melodramatic. He adds to Breihof's description, furthering his opinion that Mary was not a proper woman.

52 *"[I wanted] to make sure she understood":* Soper, "Curious Career," 705.

CHAPTER 7

53 *At the appointed time:* Soper, "Curious Career," 705.

54 *"Mary was angry":* Ibid.

"We explained our suspicions": Soper, "Typhoid Mary," 7.

Mary ranted and swore . . . not from her: Soper, "Curious Career," 705.

4,476 cases: Annual Report, 473.

55 *Mary insisted that she hadn't caused:* Soper, "Typhoid Mary," 7.

Mary probably didn't understand: This conclusion is drawn from Mary's letter (hereafter cited as "Mary's letter"), her reactions to Soper and other health officials, and as concluded by Leavitt in *Typhoid Mary: Captive,* 196; and Baker, 73.

55 *According to social research:* Cass, AP GfK Poll conducted in 2012.

56 *the famous Dr. Elizabeth Blackwell:* Elston.

as high as 96 percent . . . 51 percent who: Swanson, "Americans Have Little Faith in Scientists," huffingtonpost.com, December 21, 2013; "Honesty/Ethics in Professions," Gallup.com, December 5–8, 2013.

57 *as many as 79 percent:* "Trust in Government," Gallup.com.

58 *"a volley of imprecations":* Soper, "Curious Career," 705.

"We were glad to close": Soper, "Typhoid Mary," 7.

Once again, he had explained: Ibid., 6.

59 *If Mary quit:* Soper, "Curious Career," 705.

60 *called Mary "a living culture tube"... "it was impossible":* Ibid.

"If the Department meant": Ibid.

61 *Bill of Rights*: Bill of Rights Institute. billofrightsinstitute.org/founding documents/bill-of-rights (accessed November 4, 2014).

62 *But no individual's civil and legal rights:* Mary's case would not set any legal precedent. It took until 1925 and the precedent-setting case of *Gitlow v. People* (or *Gitlow v. New York*) for the U.S. Supreme Court to find that individual state governments could not abridge the First Amendment, which guarantees freedom of speech. In later years, other U.S. Supreme Court cases would establish precedents for other amendments in the Bill of Rights. I am grateful to my husband, Joe—and to the thirty years he spent teaching political history—for alerting me to this case.

These laws require: West, telephone interviews by author, April 21, 2014, and July 12, 2014.

63 *"legislative, judicial, and executive powers":* Biggs, 371.

"I do not think": Ibid.

"It shall be the duty": Birdseye, 465.

64 *And Biggs knew just the woman:* Baker, 73.

Chapter 8

65 *"I learned afterward":* Baker, 73.

She had lost her father: Ibid., 24–25. The Poughkeepsie water supply was blamed for the typhoid epidemic. This resulted in the installation of the first American filtration plant for a town's water supply.

66 *Baker was one of the few female physicians:* Parry.

understood the connection: "Changing the Face of Medicine."

Tenement House Act: Gilbert, 446. Before 1901, doctors attributed eight thousand to nine thousand deaths a year to tuberculosis, mostly in the tenement districts. The city's leading physicians—Hermann Biggs, included—pushed for improvements. The Tenement House Act, however, infuriated landlords. In 1900 the New York City death rate was 20.57 per 1,000. At that time, there were 82,652 tenement houses in New York City. The new law required landlords to improve the buildings that had been perfectly legal before the act passed on April 11, 1901. At their own expense, landlords had to supply indoor toilets, windows for each room, fire escapes, hall lights, a skylight, and waterproof cellars. The new laws were even tougher for new construction, which required buildings to have rooms of a minimum square footage, fireproof stairs and entry halls, and specified window size. Furthermore, new buildings could occupy no more than 70 percent of the lot. See also www.livingcityarchive.org/htm/framesets/themes/tenements/fs_1901.htm.

67 *"I climbed stair after stair":* Baker, 58.

68 *"incredibly shiftless":* Ibid., 57.

"self-respecting" woman: Ibid., 75.

"She said it in a way": Ibid., 75–76.

"Obviously, here was another case": Ibid., 74.

69 *Baker may have felt:* Keating, A17.

man-tailored suits: Baker, 64.

69 *"I doubled my fist":* Ibid., 49.

"He was in the way": Ibid., 50.

"I was not glad": Ibid., 50.

70 *in time to swear at her:* Ibid., 51.

an ambulance and three policemen: Ibid., 74.

"We were to go": Ibid.

That night it snowed: Keating, A17.

71 *"a long kitchen fork in her hand":* Baker, 74; Keating, A17. Here, the two accounts vary slightly. In 1932 Baker told Keating that Mary had a kitchen fork in her hand as she let Baker and the policeman in and then recognized them. Like Soper, Baker later gives a melodramatic account in her 1939 autobiography, writing that Mary answered the door wielding the large kitchen fork "like a rapier" and that she had "a glint in her eye."

This time it was Mary: Baker, 74.

"By the time we got through the door": Ibid., 74.

The search party moved: Baker, 75; Keating, A17.

72 *"It was utter defeat":* Baker, 75.

"I expect you to get": Ibid., 74.

"We went through every closet": Ibid., 75.

73 *A tiny fold of blue calico:* Baker, 75; Keating, A17.

"liked that loyalty": Baker, 74.

"She came out fighting": Ibid., 75.

never had typhoid: Ibid.

Mary kicked and screamed: Ibid.

74 *"It was like being in a cage":* Ibid.

"The hardest dollars I ever earned": Keating, A17.

Chapter 9

75 *screamed and kicked and swore:* Baker, 75.

sequestered in an outside isolation ward: Soper, "Curious Career," 707.

She was not allowed: New York American, "'Human Typhoid Germ' in Bellevue," 2.

76 *The hospital was a teaching facility: Transactions of the New York Academy of Medicine,* 240; Dancis and Parks, iv.

"a dangerous and unreliable person": Ibid. Soper's retellings of Mary's case grow more dramatic and harsh over the years, leaving little doubt that he felt no sympathy for her.

"If Mary had let me": Baker, 75.

77 *attendants collected the urine:* Soper, "Curious Career," 705.

The intestinal tract: Than, June 1, 2006; Dr. Cindy Corpier, email correspondence.

billions of microbes: Encyclopedia Britannica Online, "feces (biology)."

78 *kidneys create urine:* Zasloff, no page.

30 percent of the solid matter: Park, "Typhoid Bacilli Carriers," 981.

"The cook was virtually a living culture tube": Soper, "Typhoid Mary," 9. Soper's accounts show that he liked to be right—and to be acknowledged as an expert. See page 109.

79 *colonized in the gallbladder: New York Times,* "Clues to Typhoid Mary Mystery."

80 *as sick as someone who has the disease: New York American,* "Germs of Typhoid Carried for Life," 4; Nichols and Kelser, 13.

"We have here, in my judgment": Soper, "Chronic Typhoid Germ Distributor," 2022.

"*I've come to talk":* Soper, "Curious Career," 707. Soper says that Mary was held at Willard Packer for several weeks, but newspaper accounts say that her stay there was several days.

"When I have asked you": Soper, "Curious Career," 707.

81 *"You would not be":* Ibid.

Mary glared at him: Ibid. Soper says that Mary's eyes "gleamed angrily at him."

"Nobody wants to harm you": Soper, "Curious Career," 707.

why had she been kidnapped: Mary's letter.

"You say you have never caused": Soper, "Curious Career," 707.

82 *"I'll tell you how you do it":* Ibid.

83 *"The best way to get rid":* Ibid.

Your gallbladder is a small organ: "Body Maps: Gallbladder," Healthline.

they were trying to murder her: Mary's letter; *New York American,* "Typhoid Mary Never Ill, Begs Freedom," 3.

Two of the most famous serial murderers: Jenkins.

84 *"If you will answer my questions":* Soper, "Curious Career," 708.

"I will do more than you think": Ibid.

"The information would help many": Soper, "Typhoid Mary," 8.

85 *Mary stood, pulling her white bathrobe:* Soper, "Curious Career," 708.

Without uttering a word: Soper, "Curious Career," 708; Soper, "Typhoid Mary," 8. Soper says "she retreated with dignity to the toilet."

"There was no need": Soper, "Curious Career," 708.

CHAPTER 10

86 *"well-known member":* *New York American,* "'Human Typhoid Germ' in Bellevue," 2.

"HUMAN TYPHOID GERM!": Ibid. Mary was in the quarantine hospital Willard Parker.

86-7 *daily circulation of 300,000: N. W. Ayer and Son's American Newspaper Annual,* 605. The circulation of Hearst's Sunday edition, *American* and *Journal,* was 778,205 and his *Evening Journal,* 700,000. For the sake of comparison, the *New York Times* had a daily circulation of 100,000 and the *Tribune,* 65,850.

87 *"yellow journalism":* "U.S. Diplomacy and Yellow Journalism, 1895–1898." The comic strip artist Richard F. Outcault created the popular *Hogan's Alley,* about life in the slums of New York City. The comic strip was published in color in Pulitzer's *New York World,* and the character became known as "the Yellow Kid." In 1896 Hearst hired the comic strip artist away from Pulitzer, leading to a bitter battle between the two publishers. Hearst won.

"human typhoid germ": New York American, "'Human Typhoid Germ' in Bellevue," 2.

"She is practically a human vehicle": Ibid.

88 *"Mary Ilverson":* Ibid.

"she constantly makes attempts": Ibid.

federal law provides statutes: O'Connor and Matthews.

The most common law: Ibid. See also Rosenbaum, Abramson, and MacTaggert, 116–21.

89 *"This woman is a great menace": New York American,* "'Human Typhoid Germ' in Bellevue," 2.

90 *typhoid fever was a national crisis: Mortality Statistics,* 35. This source states that 30.3 deaths occurred per 100,000. In 1907 the U.S. population was 87 million.

Many Americans believed: Leavitt, *Typhoid Mary: Captive,* 6.

The disease causes skin sores: "Leprosy," MedlinePlus.

91 *certain communicable diseases*: "Questions and Answers on the Executive Order Adding Potentially Pandemic Influenza Viruses to the List of Quarantinable Diseases." Centers for Disease Control and Prevention, cdc.gov, May 30, 2014.

"The zephyrs will come along": Plunkett, 3.

92 *"Said board [of health] may remove":* Birdseye, 465.

93 *Mary Mallon was packed off: New York Sun,* "Typhoid Mary in Court," 3.

CHAPTER 11

95 *"garden spot":* Riis, 417–18. Known for his documentation of the living and working conditions of the poor, Riis provides a brief history of Riverside Hospital and North Brother Island.

Isolated from the other patients: New York Sun, "Typhoid Mary in Court," 3.

"a woman who had served": Leavitt, *Typhoid Mary: Captive,* 261, fn. 19.

the emotional stress of her arrest: Mary's letter.

"When I first came here": Ibid. The six-page letter is written in her own hand and addressed to "Editor of the New York American," which is then crossed out and replaced in different handwriting with the name of her attorney, George Francis O'Neill.

96 *no eye specialist examined her:* Ibid.

The twitching may have been caused: I thank Rachel Vail's husband, Dr. Mitchell Elkind, neurology professor at Columbia University, New York City, for answering my questions about Mary's symptoms.

"my eye got better": Mary's letter.

Two or three times a week: Leavitt, *Typhoid Mary: Captive,* 32. Leavitt points out that over the next twenty-eight months, 120 of the 163 cultures (roughly 75 percent) tested positive. Forty-three cultures (26 percent) tested negative. Mary's urine was consistently negative. This indicates that she was an intermittent carrier.

97 *"I took the urotropin":* Mary's letter.

The medication was administered: Online Medical Dictionary. Today, Urotropin is known as hexamethylenetetramine. It is a powerful antibacterial agent commonly prescribed to treat urinary tract infections.

One doctor called anti-autotox: Caillé, 484.

98 *"Anything that will kill": New York Times,* "Typhoid Mary Has Reappeared," SM3.

"The danger from the typhoid carrier": Ibid.

98 *"I'm a little afraid":* Mary's letter

The hospital permitted visitors: Riis, 419.

99 *"A keeper, three times a day": New York American,* "Typhoid Mary Never Ill, Begs Freedom," 3.

"They do not dread": New York Call, "Typhoid Mary Again at Large," 1.

Mary had made a close friend: Leavitt, *Typhoid Mary: Captive,* 183.

"Often I help nurse": New York World, "I'm Persecuted! Is Plaintive Plea of Typhoid Mary," 18.

"I never had typhoid": New York American, "Typhoid Mary: Most Harmless Yet Most Dangerous Woman in America," 6–7.

100 *"Naturally, I said New York":* Mary's letter.

"So there was a stop": Ibid.

When the supervising nurse: Ibid.

"Well, I have no sister": Ibid.

101 *"I have been told": New York World,* "I'm Persecuted!" Is Plaintive Plea of Typhoid Mary," 18.

August Breihof served as courier: Breihof's name and address are found on the Ferguson Laboratory reports, filed "In the Matter of . . . Mary Mallon."

On visitation day, Breihof rode: Riis, 419.

102 *"This specimen gives negative results":* Ferguson Laboratory reports.

Mary's specimens tested positive: Leavitt, *Typhoid Mary: Captive,* 32.

It's also possible: Dr. Cindy Corpier, email interview; see also Leavitt, *Typhoid Mary: Captive,* 32.

103 *"I cannot let her go":* Mary's letter. This confirms that the New York City Board of Health didn't want the responsibility of her release.

"do the cutting": Ibid.

she could not trust doctors: Ibid.

103 *"The Health Department just wants to use": New York American,* "Typhoid Mary Never Ill, Begs Freedom," 3. See also Walker, 21. The health department admitted that it experimented with Mary's medications.

104 *"Would it not be better":* Mary's letter.

her condition might stay the same: See Dr. M. J. Rosenau's comments in Park, 982.

typhoid bacilli can also be found: Gonzalez-Escobedo, Marshall, and Gunn, 1.

"I understand that the gall bladder": New York Times, "Typhoid Mary Has Reappeared," SM3.

105 *"The case of this woman":* Park, 981.

106 *"except as in the case":* Ibid., 982.

CHAPTER 12

107 *"'Typhoid Mary' Most Harmless": New York American,* "Typhoid Mary: Most Harmless Yet Most Dangerous Woman in America," 6–7.

108 *boasted a circulation of nearly 800,000: N. W. Ayer and Sons American Newspaper Annual,* 605. The circulation numbers are missing in *Ayer's* for 1909. Two years earlier, *Ayer's* gives the circulation number as 778, 205, or nearly 800,000.

"Every effort has been made": New York American, "Typhoid Mary: Most Harmless Yet Most Dangerous Woman in America," 6–7.

"It is probable": Ibid.

109 *"I have been in fact a peep show":* Mary's letter. The undated letter was never published.

"I wonder how the said Dr.": Ibid.

"absurd": Ibid. The word can be found on the last page in O'Neill's handwritten note.

There is no evidence: Leavitt, *Typhoid Mary: Captive,* 279, fn. 15.

110 *"[They] were moved by pity": New York American,* "Typhoid Mary Never Ill, Begs Freedom," 7.

filed a legal complaint: "In the Matter of . . . Mary Mallon." The exact chronology of the events is not clear. Some say that O'Neill learned about Mary's situation from the *New York American* article published on June 20, 1909. The court document itself states that O'Neill filed the writ on or about June 28, 1909. It also seems reasonable to conclude that the *New York American* interviewed O'Neill and that he used the interview to elicit support for Mary's case. The results, however, remain the same, regardless of the order: The *New York American* learned of Mary's identity and was the first to break the story. O'Neill offered to represent her, and he filed the writ.

111 *In her dress pocket she carried: New York American,* "Typhoid Mary Never Ill, Begs Freedom," 7.

"She has a clear, healthy complexion": Ibid.

"as rosy as you please": New York Sun, "Typhoid Mary in Court," 3.

Reporters also used language: Chicago Inter Ocean, "Typhoid Prisoner Asks Her Freedom," 5; *Norwood News,* "Typhoid Radiator Wants Freedom," 5; *New York Times,* "Typhoid Mary Must Stay," 3. In 1915, the *Tacoma Times* would call her a "witch" outright.

112 *"one of the few freaks": Chicago Inter Ocean,* "Typhoid Prisoner Asks Her Freedom," 5.

Skulls rose from the steam: New York American, "Typhoid Mary Never Ill, Begs Freedom," 7.

"had a right to examine": Mary's letter. These words appear in O'Neill's handwritten note on the last page of the letter.

"I am an innocent": New York American, "Typhoid Mary, Never Ill, Begs Freedom," 7.

113 *"If the mere statement": New York Evening Post,* "Typhoid Mary," 1.

4,426 new cases: Annual Report, 1908, 603. In 1908, there were 536 deaths.

"This woman has been a victim": Ibid.

114 *five healthy carriers:* Leavitt, *Typhoid Mary: Captive,* 88.

fifty carriers: New York American, "Typhoid Mary: Most Harmless Yet Most Dangerous Woman in America," 6.

"Her occupation as a cook": "In the Matter . . . of Mary Mallon."

did not broker a deal: This is evident from Mary's letter and other facts of her case. Leavitt also makes this point in "A Menace to the Community."

115 *new science of bacteriology* and *no witnesses testified:* Leavitt, *Typhoid Mary,* 72.

"Where would we put them": New York Tribune, "Has New York Many Walking Pesthouses?," 5.

116 *Some medical professionals:* Mason, 118.

"New Thought Student": New York Times, "To the Editor of the New York Times," 6.

"If Miss Mallon is not over ten": New York American, "Typhoid Mary Has Offer to Become Bride," 2.

117 *"One thing she should": New York American,* "Ban on Typhoid Mary," 5.

"While the court deeply sympathizes": New York Times, "Typhoid Mary Must Stay," 3.

"two kinds of justice": New York World, "I'm Persecuted! Is Plaintive Plea of Typhoid Mary," 18.

"All the water": Ibid.

118 *"As there is a God in Heaven":* Ibid.

Chapter 13

119 *"violently threatening":* Winslow, 199. Considering that Soper comments on her letter writing and later recognized her handwriting, I reason that Mary wrote violently threatening letters to Soper, too.

take a gun: Keating, A17.

119 *"I could not blame her":* Baker, 76.

"She could write an excellent letter": Soper, "Curious Career," 698.

120 "*TYPHOID MARY FREED":* *New York Times,* "Typhoid Mary Freed," 18.

"I shall change said occupation": Leavitt, *Typhoid Mary: Captive,* 189. In fn. 70, p. 305, Leavitt says that Mary Mallon agreed to let Lederle know her whereabouts every three months.

121 *"She had not been cured":* *New York American,* "Typhoid Mary Is Free; Wants Work," 6.

"As long as she observes them": *New York Times,* "Typhoid Mary Freed," 18.

"What will she do now?": Ibid.

"She is a good cook": Ibid.

122 *"She was incarcerated":* *New York American,* "Typhoid Mary Is Free," 6.

"She has been a great service": Baker, 76.

123 *washing clothes was physically demanding:* Sutherland, 92.

average life expectancy: Leonhardt.

read a great deal: Soper, "Curious Career," 698; Walker, 24.

"GUIDE A WALKING TYPHOID FACTORY": *New York Times,* "Guide a Walking Typhoid Factory," 6.

124 *She helped him:* Soper, "Curious Career," 709.

Mary turned to her attorney: *New York American,* "'Typhoid Mary,' on Island 3 Years, Sues for $50,000," sec. 4, 6.

"her chances of making": *New York Times,* "'Typhoid Mary' Asks $50,000 from City," 9.

"will demonstrate just how far": *New York American,* "'Typhoid Mary,' on Island 3 Years," sec. 4, 6.

125 *"It is quite a problem":* Ibid.

"If the Board of Health": Ibid.

125 *"no right for a civil action": New York Sun,* "Typhoid Mary Drops Her Suit," 4. For an explanation, see *Gitlow v. People* in note on page 187.

126 *Mary's case was now known: New York Times,* "Doctors Describe Disease Carriers," 6.

"It is reported": New York Times, "Typhoid Carriers," C2. On September 20, 1913, the *New York Sun* reported thirty-six cases of typhoid on New York City's East Side. At first a carrier was suspected, but then the source was determined to be contaminated milk.

CHAPTER 14

128 *Twenty-five typhoid cases: New York Tribune,* "Typhoid Mary Reappears," 8.

Sloane Hospital had an outstanding: Soper, "Typhoid Mary," 10.

129 *The Board of Health had checked:* Keating, A17.

"about a matter": Soper, "Curious Career," 710.

the hospital had hired a new cook: Ibid.

130 *Her name was Mrs. Brown:* Ibid., 11.

The other employees had teased: Ibid.

"I saw at once": Soper, "Curious Career," 698. Soper describes her handwriting on page 710.

"Sure enough, there was Mary": Baker, 76.

131 *a faint trace: New York Sun,* "Exile for Life May Be the Fate of 'Typhoid Mary,'" 1.

"which she had lovingly prepared": New York Tribune, "Typhoid Mary, Germ Carrier," 7; Walker, 22.

132 *Another officer found a ladder: New York Sun,* "Exile for Life May Be the Fate of 'Typhoid Mary,'" 1.

"The dogs offered": Ibid.

cowering in the bathroom: Ibid.

132 *"She was as strong as ever":* Soper, "Curious Career," 710.

133 *"This time she had to go back":* Baker, 76, 77.

Mary Brown and Marie Breshof and Mary Breihof: Soper, "Curious Career," 709–10.

134 *"Mary is not feeble": New York Times,* "Typhoid Mary Has Reappeared," SM3.

"She has had the assurance": Ibid.

"The chance was given to her": New York Tribune, "Typhoid Mary Reappears," 8.

"Here she was": New York Times, "Typhoid Mary Has Reappeared," SM3.

"uses far more scientific": Tacoma Times, "Witch in N.Y.," 1.

135 *"I think that if she could": New York Times,* "Typhoid Mary Has Reappeared," SM3.

"She had been given her liberty": Soper, "Typhoid Mary," 11.

Soper was angry: New York Times, "Typhoid Mary Has Reappeared," SM3.

"She has never given me": Ibid.

"the world was not very kind": Soper, "Curious Career," 709.

Chapter 15

136 *"a moody, caged jungle cat":* Walker, 23.

"Into Mary went a billion germs": Ibid.

137 *"The doctors admit":* Ibid.

In some cases: Ibid.

"In any event, Mary didn't like": Ibid. Walker's article infuriated George Soper. He called it "flippant" and "without pretense of accuracy" and said the article robbed him of credit for the discovery of the first healthy typhoid carrier to be found in America. See Soper's

letter to the editor, "The Discovery of Typhoid Mary," *British Medical Journal,* 37.

137 *"For a long time":* Leavitt, *Typhoid Mary: Captive,* 192–93.

138 *She read such magazines:* Walker, 24.

a farm worker named Tony Labella: New York Times, "Say Man Spreads Typhoid," 18; *New York Times,* "Watch for Typhoid Fever Carrier," 22; Leavitt, *Typhoid Mary: Captive,* 119.

139 *"preparing a strawberry shortcake": New York Times,* "Baker, Warned as Typhoid Carrier," 19.

"I could not legally sentence": New York Times, "Typhoid Carrier Freed," 13. Leavitt mentions a few other typhoid carriers who stayed on North Brother Island, but she notes that they never achieved the notoriety that Mary did. See Leavitt, *Typhoid Mary: Captive,* 121.

Frederick Moersch had been identified: New York American, "Typhoid Hits Village with 23 Stricken," 1, 26. See also Leavitt, *Typhoid Mary: Captive,* 121–24. Other writers, such as Stanley Walker, claim that Moersch infected 110 and caused at least six deaths.

140 *"During the years she was at large":* Baker, 76.

141 *she made new friends:* Leavitt, *Typhoid Mary: Captive,* 193.

a laboratory worker noted: Sherman, "Typhoid Mary," BBC *Timewatch,* transcript, 28.

142 *Mary worked her way up:* Leavitt, *Typhoid Mary: Captive,* 193–94.

a new resident physician: "Typhoid Mary," BBC *Timewatch,* transcript, 28.

For this, she earned: Leavitt, *Typhoid Mary: Captive,* 307, fn. 90. The details of her work are found in "Typhoid Mary," BBC *Timewatch,* transcript, and in Walker, 23.

"She was not brilliant": Walker, 23.

"She was a part of the family": Efros, "Typhoid Mary," BBC *Timewatch,* transcript, 29.

143 *a "beautiful person":* as quoted in Leavitt, *Typhoid Mary: Captive,* 194.

143 *"It's a horrible thing":* Efros, "Typhoid Mary," BBC *Timewatch,* transcript, 13.

"She was always there": Sherman, "Typhoid Mary," BBC *Timewatch,* transcript, 31.

144 *"Even though she had a stroke":* Efros, "Typhoid Mary," BBC *Timewatch,* transcript, 33.

145 *"I remember the cemetery":* Ibid., 34.

Afterword

147 *She had saved more than $4,800:* See Mallon, Mary's last will and testament.

148 *It angered George Soper:* Soper, "Discovery of Typhoid Mary," 37.

149 *A genuine interest: New York Times,* "New York's Sewage Problem a Hard One to Handle," SM13. "Do people ever stop to realize, I wonder, that life on this planet depends on three kinds of things; first, air and food; secondly, clothing and shelter; and thirdly, not a bit less important than the others, the disposal of waste matter of all kinds so that animal and vegetable life that are known as bacteria may not multiply to the destruction of human life."

150 *"Because of her confinement": New York Times,* obituary, June 18, 1948, 23.

151 *Baker died in 1945: New York Times,* "Dr. Baker Is Dead," February 23, 1945, 17.

152 *North Brother Island:* Cole, "How to Get to North Brother Island." According to a letter I received from the New York City Department of Parks and Recreation, North Brother Island is undergoing a natural restoration project from 2013 through 2016. The project will secure hazardous conditions, clean up debris, and restore the harbor heron habitat.

BIBLIOGRAPHY

Understanding Mary: In Her Own Words

Mallon, Mary. Mary's letter to the *New York American,* undated, written in her own hand, is filed with the papers "In the Matter of the Application for a Writ of Habeas Corpus for the Production of Mary Mallon," New York Supreme Court (June 28–July 22, 1909), Return to Writ. Filed at the New York County Courthouse, New York City. Mary's death certificate is held in the Bureau of Records, Department of Health of the City of New York. Mary's last will and testament is housed at the Bronx County Surrogate's Court, Bronx, New York.

Understanding Mary: From the Words of Others

Baker, S. Josephine. *Fighting for Life.* New York: Macmillan, 1939.

Edington, George, as quoted in Judith Walzer Leavitt. *Typhoid Mary: Captive to the Public's Health.* Boston: Beacon Press, 1996.

Efros, Julie. "Typhoid Mary." BBC *Timewatch,* episode 13. December 18, 1994. Transcript. Available from the BBC Written Archives.

Keating, Isabelle. "Dr. Baker Tells How She Got Her Woman." *Brooklyn Eagle* (New York), May 8, 1932, Sunday edition, sec. A17.

Mason, W. P. "Typhoid Mary." *Science,* n.s. 30, no. 760 (July 23, 1909): 117–18.

Park, William H. "Typhoid Bacilli Carriers." *Journal of the American Medical Association* 51 (1908): 981–82.

Rosenau, M. J. "Typhoid Bacilli Carriers." *Journal of the American Medical Association* 51 (1908): 982.

Sherman, Emma Rose (Goldberg). "Typhoid Mary." BBC *Timewatch,* episode 13. December 18, 1994. Transcript. Available from the BBC Written Archives.

Soper, George A. "The Curious Career of Typhoid Mary." *Bulletin of the New York Academy of Medicine* 45, no. 1 (October 1939): 698–712.

———. "The Discovery of Typhoid Mary." *British Medical Journal* (January 7, 1939): 37–38.

———. "Typhoid Mary." *Military Surgeon* 45 (July 1919): 1–15.

———. "The Work of a Chronic Typhoid Germ Distributor." *Journal of the American Medical Association* 48 (1907): 2019–22.

Walker, Stanley. "Profiles 'Typhoid Carrier No. 36.'" *New Yorker,* January 26, 1935, 21–25.

Wenzell, Thomas. "Typhoid Mary." BBC *Timewatch,* episode 13. December 18, 1994. Transcript. Available from the BBC Written Archives.

Winslow, C.E.A. *The Life of Hermann M. Biggs, M.D., D.Sc., L.L.D.: Physician and Statesman of the Public Health.* Philadelphia: Lea and Febiger, 1929.

Understanding Mary from Newspaper Accounts

Chicago Inter Ocean. "Typhoid Prisoner Asks Her Freedom." June 30, 1909.

New York American. "Ban on Typhoid Mary." July 23, 1909. Print.

———. "Germs of Typhoid Carried for Life." March 13, 1907.

———. "Healthy Disease Spreaders." July 1, 1909. Print.

———. "'Human Typhoid Germ' in Bellevue." April 2, 1907. Print.

———. "Typhoid Hits Village, with 23 Stricken." October 7, 1928.

———. "Typhoid Mary Has Offer to Become Bride." July 21, 1909.

———. "Typhoid Mary Is Free; Wants Work." February 21, 1910. Print.

———. "Typhoid Mary: Most Harmless Yet Most Dangerous Woman in America." June 20, 1909.

———. "Typhoid Mary Never Ill, Begs Freedom." June 30, 1909.

———. "'Typhoid Mary,' on Island 3 Years, Sues for $50,000." December 3, 1911.

New York Call. "Typhoid Mary Again at Large." February 21, 1910.

New York Evening Post. "Typhoid Mary." July 16, 1909.

New York Sun. "Exile for Life May Be Fate of 'Typhoid Mary.'" March 28, 1915.

———. "Typhoid Mary Drops Her Suit." December 31, 1917.

———. "Typhoid Mary in Court." June 30, 1909.

New York Times. "Baker, Warned as Typhoid Carrier, in Court as Public Menace for Making Shortcake." March 14, 1924.

———. "Clues to Typhoid Mary Mystery." August 7, 2013.

———. "Died." February 24, 1907.

———. "Doctors Describe Disease Carriers." September 26, 1912.

———. "Five Ill in One Household: Typhoid Attacks Charles E. Warren's Family and Servants." September 11, 1906.

———. "Guide a Walking Typhoid Factory." December 2, 1910.

———. "New York's Sewage Problem a Hard One to Handle." December 25, 1910.

———. "Say Man Spreads Typhoid." October 13, 1922.

———. "To the Editor of the New York Times." July 2, 1909.

———. "Typhoid Carrier Freed." March 15, 1924.

———. "Typhoid Carriers." November 29, 1914.

———. "'Typhoid Mary' Asks $50,000 from City." December 3, 1911.

———. "Typhoid Mary Freed." February 21, 1910.

———. "Typhoid Mary Has Reappeared." April 4, 1915, sec. Sunday Magazine.

———. "Typhoid Mary Must Stay." July 17, 1909.

———. "Watch for Typhoid Fever Carrier." January 21, 1923.

New York Tribune. "Has New York Many Walking Pesthouses?" July 4, 1909. Print.

———. "Typhoid Mary, Germ Carrier." March 28, 1915.

———. "Typhoid Mary Reappears." March 29, 1915.

New York World. "I'm Persecuted! Is Plaintive Plea of Typhoid Mary." July 20, 1909.

Norwood News (St. Lawrence, N.Y.). "Typhoid Radiator Wants Freedom." August 17, 1909.

Tacoma Times (Washington). "Witch in N.Y." April 6, 1915.

Understanding Mary, Secondary Sources

Bourdain, Anthony. *Typhoid Mary: An Urban Historical.* New York: Bloomsbury, USA, 2001.

Hammond, John E. "Typhoid Mary." In *Oyster Bay Remembered.* Oyster Bay, New York: Maple Hill Press, 2002.

Leavitt, Judith Walzer. "A Menace to the Community." www.learner.org

/workshops/primarysources/disease/docs/leavitt2.html (accessed February 23, 2014).

———. *Typhoid Mary: Captive to the Public's Health*. Boston: Beacon Press, 1996.

———. "Typhoid Mary Strikes Back: Bacteriological Theory and Practice in Early 20th-Century Public Health." In *Sickness and Health in America: Readings in the History of Medicine and Public Health*. Madison: University of Wisconsin Press, 1997.

Lovering, Mrs. (no first name). "Typhoid Mary." BBC *Timewatch,* episode 13. December 18, 1994. Transcript. Available from the BBC Written Archives.

Mendelsohn, J. Andrew. "'Typhoid Mary' Strikes Again: The Social and the Scientific in the Making of Modern Public Health." *Isis* 86, no. 2 (June 1995): 268–77.

Wald, Priscilla. *Contagious: Cultures, Carriers, and the Outbreak Narrative*. Durham, N.C.: Duke University Press, 2008.

Understanding Mary's World

Amsterdam, Daniel. "Down and Out (Again): America's Long Struggle with Mass Unemployment." *Origins: Current Events in Historical Perspective*. origins.osu.edu/article/down-and-out-again-america-s-long-struggle-mass-unemployment (accessed April 27, 2014).

Blessing, Patrick J. "Irish." In *Harvard Encyclopedia of American Ethnic Groups,* edited by Steven Thernstrom. Cambridge: Harvard University Press, 1980.

Branch, Enobong Hannah, and Melissa E. Wooten. "Suited for Service: Racialized Rationalizations for the Ideal Domestic Servant from the Nineteenth to the Early Twentieth Century." *Social Science History* 36, no. 2 (2012): 169–89.

Cassell's Household Guide to Every Department of Practical Life: Being a Complete Encyclopaedia of Domestic and Social Economy. New and rev. ed. London: Cassell, 1895.

Census reports. Tenth census. June 1, 1880. Washington, D.C.: U.S. Department of Congress, 188388.

Cole, Sean. "How to Get to North Brother Island." *Radiolab Blogland.* November 15, 2011. Accessed November 18, 2014. www.radiolab.org/story/170476-how-get-north-brother-island.

Davis, Stephen. "The Great Horse Manure Crisis of 1884." *The Freeman: Ideas on Liberty.* September 1, 2004. Accessed November 18, 2014. fee.org/files/doclib/547_32.pdf.

Douglas, Paul H., and Aaron Director. *The Problem of Unemployment.* New York: Macmillan, 1931.

"Early 20th Century American Kitchens." Kitchens from 1900 to 1920. www.antiquehomestyle.com/inside/kitchen/1900–20/index.htm (accessed February 24, 2014).

Ehrenreich, Barbara, and Deidre English. *For Her Own Good: Two Centuries of the Experts' Advice to Women.* New York: Anchor Books, Random House, 2005.

Flanagan, Shaun. "Burke and Hare." Edinburgh Body Snatchers, www.edinburgh-history.co.uk/burke-hare.html (accessed March 11, 2014).

Gilbert, Judith A. "Tenements and Takings: Tenement House Department of New York v. Moeschen as a Counterpoint to Lochner v. New York." *Fordham Urban Law Journal* 18, no. 3 (1990): 446. ir.lawnet.fordham.edu/cgi/viewcontent.cgi?article=1346&context=ulj (accessed March 9, 2014).

Gore, Thomas, DVM, Paula Gore, and James M. Giffin, MD. *Horse Owner's Veterinary Handbook.* Third ed. Hoboken, N.J.: Howell Book House, Wiley Publishing, 2008.

Gregory, Annie R. *Woman's Favorite Cookbook.* Chicago: Monarch Book Company, 1902.

Harris-Perry, Melissa V. *Sister Citizen: Shame, Stereotypes, and Black Women in America.* Reprint. New Haven: Yale University Press, 2013.

Hill, Daniel Delis. *Advertising to the American Woman, 1900–1999.* Columbus: Ohio State University Press, 2002.

Husband, Julie, and Jim O'Loughlin. *Daily Life in the Industrial United States, 1870–1900.* Westport, Conn.: Greenwood Press, 2004.

Jenkins, John. "William Burke and William Hare (Irish criminals)." *Encyclopaedia Britannica Online.* www.britannica.com/EBchecked/topic/1345659/William-Burke-and-William-Hare (accessed February 23, 2014).

Johnson, Allan. *Privilege, Power, and Difference.* Boston: McGraw-Hill, 2006.

Katzman, David M. *Seven Days a Week: Women and Domestic Service in Industrializing America.* New York: Oxford University Press, 1978.

Leonhardt, David. "Life Expectancy Data." *New York Times.* www.nytimes.com/2006/09/27/business/27leonhardt_sidebar.html?_r=0 (accessed September 27, 2006).

Lynch-Brennan, Margaret. *The Irish Bridget: Irish Immigrant Women in Domestic Service in America, 1840–1930.* New York: Syracuse University Press, 2009.

"Measuring Worth—Relative Worth Calculators and Data Sets." www.measuringworth.com (accessed February 24, 2014).

Melosi, Martin V. *Garbage in the Cities: Refuse, Reform, and the Environment.* Rev. ed. Pittsburgh: University of Pittsburgh Press, 2005.

"Movements for Political & Social Reform, 1870–1914." MultiText Project in Irish History. multitext.ucc.ie/d/Ireland_society_economy_1870-1914 (accessed February 21, 2014).

New York City directory, 1903–1908.

New York Times. "Women Discuss Ice Question." May 18, 1900, 2.

Perlman, Joel. *Ethnic Difference: Schooling and Social Structure Among the Irish, Italians, Jews & Blacks in an American City, 1880–1935.* New York: Cambridge University Press, 1988.

Plunkett, H. M. *Women, Plumbers, and Doctors, or, Household Sanitation.* New York: Appleton, 1897.

"The Quality of the Oldsmobile." *The Motor Way.* July 5, 1906.

Riis, Jacob. "The Riverside Hospital." In *The Annals of Hygiene.* Philadelphia: University of Pennsylvania Press, 1892.

Ryan, James G. *Irish Records: Sources for Family and Local History.* Dublin: Flyleaf Press, 1997.

Strasser, Susan. *Never Done: A History of American Housework.* New York: Pantheon Books, 1982.

Sutherland, Donald E. *Americans and Their Servants: Domestic Service in the United States from 1800 to 1920.* Baton Rouge: Louisiana State University Press, 1981.

Welter, Barbara. "The Cult of True Womanhood: 1820–1860." *American Quarterly* 18, no. 2 (1966): 152.

White, Erica. "Representations of the True Woman and the New Woman in *Harper's Bazaar,* 1870–1879 and 1890–1905." Graduate theses and dissertations. Paper 10695. lib.dr.iastate.edu/cgi/viewcontent.cgi?article=1676&context=etd (accessed February 22, 2014).

Understanding George Soper and Josephine Baker

Boronson, Walter. "In Defense of Typhoid Mary." newjerseynewsroom.com.

www.newjerseynewsroom.com/healthquest/in-defense-of-typhoid-mary (accessed March 11, 2014).

"Changing the Face of Medicine: Dr. S. Josephine Baker." U.S. National Library of Medicine. www.nlm.nih.gov/changingthefaceofmedicine/physicians/biography_19.html (accessed February 23, 2014).

Draxler, Breanna. "Teaching Kids to Think Like Engineers." *Discover Magazine,* November 5, 2013. discovermagazine.com/2013/dec/15-e-is-for-engineering#.UrXHQqXfbNA (accessed February 22, 2014).

Elston, M. A. "Blackwell, Elizabeth (1821–1910), Physician." *Oxford Dictionary of National Biography.* www.oxforddnb.com/view/printable/31912 (accessed February 22, 2014).

"Engineers Explained." bcn.boulder.co.us/~neal/engineerhumor.html (accessed February 22, 2014).

"What Are Scientists and Engineers Like?" *JPL Education.* www.jpl.nasa.gov/education/index.cfm?page=141 (accessed February 22, 2014).

UNDERSTANDING TYPHOID, HYGIENE, AND DISEASE

Bernberg, Erin L., University of Delaware and Delaware Biotechnology, Newark, Del. Telephone and email interviews by author, July 25, 2014.

"Body Maps: Gallbladder." Healthline. www.healthline.com/human-body-maps/gallbladder (accessed July 29, 2014).

The Burn Foundation. *Burn Prevention.* www.burnfoundation.org/programs/resource.cfm?c=1&a=3 (accessed February 21, 2014).

Caillé, Augustus. *Postgraduate Medicine; Prevention and Treatment of Disease.* New York: Appleton, 1922.

Corpier, Cindy, MD. Dallas Nephrology Associates, Texas. Email correspondence with the author, February 18, 2004.

Dancis, Joseph, and Wade Parks. "Introduction." *Pediatrics* 90, no. 1 (1992): iv.

"Discovery of Germs." With Dr. Kelly Reynolds at the University of Arizona. learnaboutgerms.arizona.edu/discovery_of_germs.htm (accessed February 21, 2014).

Dziura, Jennifer. "Bullish Life: When Men Are Too Emotional to Have a Rational Argument." *The Gloss* RSS. www.thegloss.com/2012/11/12/career/bullish-life-men-are-too-emotional-to-have-a-rational-argument-994/#ixzz2CnkN6Vur (accessed February 22, 2014).

Elkind, Michell, professor of neurology and epidemiology, Department of Neurology, Columbia University Medical Center, New York. Email interview by author, January 2, 2014.

Encyclopaedia Britannica Online. "feces (biology)." www.britannica.com/EBchecked/topic/203293/feces (accessed February 23, 2014).

"Epidemiology." University of Hartford. uhaweb.hartford.edu/bugl/Epidemiology.pdf (accessed February 22, 2014).

Gonzalez-Escobedo, Geoffrey, Joanna M. Marshall, and John S. Gunn. "Chronic and Acute Infections of the Gall Bladder by Salmonella Typhi: Understanding the Carrier State." *Nature Review Microbiology*. www.ncbi.nlm.nih.gov/pmc/articles/PMC3255095/ (accessed February 23, 2014).

"Leprosy." MedlinePlus. U.S. National Library of Medicine. www.nlm.nih.gov/medlineplus/ency/article/001347.htm (accessed March 9, 2014).

Long-Islander (Huntington, New York). "The Water Supply Question." November 16, 1906.

Mann, Denise. "Kitchen Germs: Stopping Germs Where They Breed." *WebMD*. www.webmd.com/food-recipes/features/germs-in-kitchen (accessed February 18, 2014).

Mayo Staff. "Typhoid Fever." Mayo Clinic. www.mayoclinic.com/health

/typhoid-fever/DS00538/DSECTION=causes (accessed February 21, 2014).

"Miasma." MedTerms. www.medterms.com/script/main/art.asp?articlekey =19304 (accessed February 22, 2014).

Mortality Statistics. Department of Commerce and Labor. S.N.D North, director. 8th Annual Report. Washington: Government Printing Office, 1909.

Nichols, Henry James, and Raymond Alexander Kelser. *Carriers in Infectious Diseases: A Manual on the Importance, Pathology, Diagnosis and Treatment of Human Carriers.* Baltimore: Williams & Wilkins, 1922.

Parry, Manon S. "Sara Josephine Baker (1873–1945)." U.S. National Library of Medicine. www.ncbi.nlm.nih.gov/pmc/articles/PMC1470556 (accessed February 23, 2014).

"Questions and Answers on the Executive Order Adding Potentially Pandemic Influenza Viruses to the List of Quarantinable Diseases." Centers for Disease Control and Prevention. www.cdc.gov/quarantine/qa-executive-order-pandemic-list-quarantinable-diseases.html (accessed October 23, 2014).

"Robert Koch—Biographical." Nobelprize.org. www.nobelprize.org /nobel_prizes/medicine/laureates/1905/koch-bio.html (accessed February 21, 2014).

"Robert Koch, 1843–1910." Open Collections Program: Contagion. ocp .hul.harvard.edu/contagion/koch.html (accessed February 21, 2014).

"S. typhi." Water Treatability Database. iaspub.epa.gov/tdb/pages/contaminant/contaminantOverview.do?contaminantId=10460 (accessed February 21, 2014).

Smith, Susan. "Teaching the History of Public Health and Health Reform." *Magazine of History* 19, no. 5 (September 2005): 27–29.

Than, Ker. "Scientists Examine 100 Trillion Microbes in Human Feces."

LiveScience. www.livescience.com/10501-scientists-examine-100-trillion-microbes-human-feces.html (accessed February 23, 2014).

Watts, Sheldon. *Epidemics and History: Disease, Power, and Imperialism.* New Haven: Yale University Press, 1997.

"What Is Urotropin?" Online Medical Dictionary. www.medicaldictionaryonline.info/medical-term/Urotropin (accessed February 23, 2014).

Zasloff, Michael. "Antimicrobial Peptides, Innate Immunity, and the Normally Sterile Urinary Tract." *Journal of the American Society of Nephrology.* jasn.asnjournals.org/content/18/11/2810.full (accessed February 23, 2014).

Understanding Public Health, the Law, and the Trust Factor

Annual Report of the Board of Health of the Department of Health of the City of New York for the Year Ending December 31, 1906. New York: Martin B. Brown, 1907.

Annual Report of the Board of Health of the City of New York for the year ending December 31, 1908. New York: Martin B. Brown, 1909.

"Beyond Typhoid Mary: The Origins of Public Health at Columbia and in the City." *Living Legacies.* www.columbia.edu/cu/alumni/Magazine/Spring2004/publichealth.html (accessed February 21, 2014).

Biggs, Hermann. "The Preventative and Administrative Measures of the Control of Tuberculosis in New York City." *Lancet* 2 (1910): 371.

Birdseye, Clarence. *The Greater New York Charter.* New York: Baker, Voorhis, and Co., 1897.

Cass, Connie. "In God We Trust, Maybe, but Not Each Other." AP GfK Poll. ap-gfkpoll.com/featured/our-latest-poll-findings-24 (accessed February 22, 2014).

DeKok, David. *The Epidemic: A Collision of Power, Privilege, and Public Health.* Guilford, Conn.: Globe Pequot Press, 2011.

Farley, Joseph, Department of Health, Lackawanna County, Scranton, Pa. Telephone interview by author, June 16, 2014.

"Gitlow v. People." Legal Information Institute. www.law.cornell.edu /supremecourt/text/268/652 (accessed February 23, 2014).

Gostin, Lawrence O. "Public Health Law Reform." U.S. National Library of Medicine. www.ncbi.nlm.nih.gov/pmc/articles/PMC1446780 (accessed April 14, 1929).

"Honesty/Ethics in Professions." Gallup.Com. www.gallup.com/poll/1654/ honesty-ethics-professions.aspx (accessed February 22, 2014).

Monk, Linda R. *The Words We Live By: Your Annotated Guide to the Constitution.* 1st ed. New York: Hyperion, 2003.

O'Connor, Jean, and Gene Matthews. "Informational Privacy, Public Health, and State Laws." National Center for Biotechnology Information. www.ncbi.nlm.nih.gov/pmc/articles/PMC3222345 (accessed April 29, 2014).

Public Health and Law Enforcement Emergency Preparedness Workgroup. "Joint Public Health–Law Enforcement Investigations: Model Memorandum of Understanding." www.nasemso.org/Projects/DomesticPrepared ness/documents/JIMOUFinal.pdf (accessed April 30, 2014).

Rosenbaum, Sara, Susan Abramson, and Patricia MacTaggart. "Health Information Law in the Context of Minors." *Pediatrics: Official Journal of the American Academy of Pediatrics.* pediatrics.aappublications .org/content/123/Supplement_2/S116.full.pdf (accessed April 30, 2014).

Swanson, Emily. "Americans Have Little Faith in Scientists, Science Journalists: Poll." *Huffington Post.* www.huffingtonpost.com/2013/12/21/faith -in-scientists_n_4481487.html (accessed October 23, 2014).

"Trust in Government." Gallup.Com. www.gallup.com/poll/5392/trust-government.aspx (accessed February 22, 2014).

West, Daniel, chairman, Department of Health Administration and Human Resources, University of Scranton, Scranton, Pa. Telephone interviews by author, April 21, 2014, and July 15, 2014.

Understanding Yellow Journalism

N. W. Ayer & Son's American Newspaper Annual. 1907 pt.1. Library of Congress. lcweb2.loc.gov/diglib/vols/loc.gdc.sr.sn91012091.00143502016/pageturner.html?page=1&submit=Go&size=800 (accessed February 23, 2014).

"U.S. Diplomacy and Yellow Journalism, 1895–1898," U.S. Department of State Office of the Historian. history.state.gov/milestones/1866–1898/yellow-journalism (accessed February 22, 2014).

The Yellow Kid. Ohio State University Libraries. cartoons.osu.edu/digital_albums/yellowkid (accessed February 25, 2014).

ACKNOWLEDGMENTS

It's always a great pleasure to thank those who have helped along the way.

I'd like to acknowledge the following people and institutions who alerted me to sources, helped me obtain sources, verified information, answered my questions, and listened to me. Rachel Vail, Dr. Mitchell Elkind, professor of neurology and epidemiology, Columbia University, New York City, for answering my questions about Mary's symptoms; Dr. Cindy Corpier, Dallas Nephrology Associates, Texas, for answering my questions about the function of the intestinal tract and laboratory reporting; Dr. Daniel West, chair, Department of Public Health, University of Scranton, Pennsylvania, for answering my questions about public health law; and Joe Farley, a registered nurse at the Lackawanna County Department of Health, Scranton, Pennsylvania, for answering my questions about reportable infectious diseases.

Chasing down sources is always part of the fun. I'm grateful to Erika Funke, WVIA Pittston, Pennsylvania, for connecting me with Fiona Powell, WVIA Williamsport, Pennsylvania, whose valiant attempts to track down the nearly impossible to find BBC transcript are duly noted; Sarah Bond, assistant curator at the Wellcome Library, London, England, for transcribing the interview portions I needed; and Jennifer Hogg at the Written Archives, BBC, for locating and sending me the entire transcript.

Thank you to the New York Public Library and its awesome reference section; the Oyster Bay Historical Society, Long Island, New York; the interlibrary loan librarians at Penn State main campus; the reference librarians at the Albright Memorial Library, Scranton, Pennsylvania; and the ever-divine Betsey Moylan at the University of Scranton Weinburg Memorial Library.

My friends have helped in immeasurable ways. Thank you, Nancy Cummings, for your great humor; Bambi Lobdell, for our many conversations that helped inform this book; and my editor, Ann Rider, and my agent, Ginger Knowlton, at Curtis Brown LTD for your support.

I am ever grateful to my family, who provide me with laughter, endless stories, opportunities for procrastination, and something to say: Brandy, Rick, Alia, Rocco, and Mia; Joe and Lyndsay; Mom; and, always and forever, Joe.

INDEX

M

R

S

U

V

W